Wonderful Discovery

The point of the horn pierced Jamie's flesh like a sword made of fire and ice. He cried out, first in pain, then in joy and wonder. Finally the answer was clear to him, and he understood his obsession and his loneliness.

"No wonder I didn't fit," he thought, as his fingers fused, then split into cloven hooves.

The transformation was painful. But the joy so far surpassed it that he barely noticed the fire he felt as his neck began to stretch and the horn erupted from his brow. "No wonder, no wonder—no, it's all wonder, wonder, wonder and joy!"

He reared back in triumph, his silken mane streaming behind him, as he trumpeted the joyful discovery that he was, and always had been, and always would be, a unicorn.

Other Avon Camelot Books
Compiled and Edited by
Bruce Coville

BRUCE COVILLE'S ALIEN VISITORS

Coming Soon

BRUCE COVILLE'S STRANGE WORLDS

BRUCE COVILLE'S
SHAPESHIFTERS

COMPILED AND EDITED BY
BRUCE COVILLE

ASSISTED BY STEVE ROMAN

Illustrated by Ernie Colón and John Nyberg

A GLC BOOK

AN AVON CAMELOT BOOK

AVON BOOKS, INC.
1350 Avenue of the Americas
New York, New York 10019

Copyright © 1999 by General Licensing Company, Inc. All rights reserved.
Cover artwork copyright © 1999 by General Licensing Company, Inc.
Cover painting by Ernie Colón
Illustrations by Ernie Colón and John Nyberg

Introduction copyright © 1999 by Bruce Coville.
"Homeward Bound" copyright © 1987 by Bruce Coville; originally published in *The Unicorn Treasury* (Doubleday) edited by Bruce Coville. Reprinted by permission of the author.
"I Was a Bestselling Teenage Werewolf" copyright © 1998 by Lawrence Watt-Evans.
"Myself" copyright © 1998 by Mark A. Garland.
"Frog Princes" copyright © 1998 by Janni Lee Simner.
"Tricky Coyote" copyright © 1998 by Susan J. Kroupa.
"Swan Sister" copyright © 1996 by Anne Mazer. Reprinted by permission of Anne Mazer from *A Sliver of Glass and Other Uncommon Tales.*
"The Changelings" copyright © 1995 by Jessica Amanda Salmonson; originally published in *Phantom Waters: Northwest Legends of Rivers, Lakes and Shores* (Sasquatch Books). Reprinted by permission of the author.
"The Talking Sword" copyright © 1998 by Jack Dann.
"Freedom" copyright © 1998 by Connie Wilkins.
"Fever Dream" copyright © 1948, renewed 1975 by Ray Bradbury. Reprinted by permission of Don Congdon Associates, Inc.
"The Electronic Werewolf" copyright © 1998 by Lael Littke and Lori Littke Silfen.
"Wilding" copyright © 1995 by Jane Yolen. First published by Harcourt Brace & Company in *A Starfarer's Dozen*, Michael Stearns, ed. Reprinted by permission of Curtis Brown, Ltd.
"Jonas. Just Jonas" copyright © 1998 by Nancy Varian Berberick and Greg LaBarbera.
"A Million Copies in Print" copyright © 1998 by John C. Bunnell.

Library of Congress Catalog Card Number: 98-93662
ISBN: 0-380-80255-4
www.avonbooks.com

First Avon Camelot Printing: October 1999

CAMELOT TRADEMARK REG. U.S. PAT. OFF. AND IN OTHER COUNTRIES, MARCA REGISTRADA, HECHO EN U.S.A.

Printed in the U.S.A.

OPM 10 9 8 7 6 5 4 3 2 1

CONTENTS

INTRODUCTION:

What shape are your dreams?

Welcome to our world of shifting forms and tales of metamorphosis!

Of course, stories about shapeshifting, or "morphing," as it is sometimes called, are hot these days—what, after all, are the Transformers, the Mighty Morphin' Power Rangers, and the Animorphs (not to mention the ever-popular werewolf) but different kinds of shapeshifters? But what you might not have realized is that while most of those characters are fairly new, the *idea* of shapeshifting has been around for longer than you might have realized—for as long, in fact, as people have been telling stories.

Zeus, the king of the Greek gods, was constantly taking on new shapes—everything from a bull to a shower of gold—to pursue whatever girl happened to strike his fancy at the moment. The Romans picked up the Greek mythology, and found in it so many tales of shapeshifting that the poet Ovid wrote an entire book called *The Metamorphosis*—poetic versions of tales about people transformed from one shape to another. In Norse mythology, the god of mischief, Loki, was a notorious shapeshifter—as are the trickster gods in most myth systems.

The trend continues today, of course, not only in fantasy, but in science fiction, with such characters as Odo in *Star Trek: Deep Space Nine*.

Obviously, this fascination with shapeshifting has lasted for several thousand years.

But why?

Well, in one sense we are all shapeshifters. We start small, weak, and wrinkled and spend the next several years changing our shape and size as we gain wisdom and power. But it's a terribly slow and sometimes painful process. No wonder people fantasize about doing it instantly.

Of course, there are times, especially in adolescence, when our shapeshifting does seem to happen almost instantly. Some kids shoot up several inches in a matter of only a few months. At the same time, our bodies change in all sorts of strange, interesting, and sometimes slightly terrifying ways. We're shapeshifters indeed during the teen years. So it makes sense that kids of that age have a special fascination with the idea.

And consider this: how many of us are ever completely satisfied with the shape we're in—especially in this culture, which is so absurdly obsessed with physical beauty? Rare indeed is the person who hasn't wanted to look like someone else—or to have the wings of an eagle, the strength of a lion, the speed of a gazelle.

What shape are *your* dreams?

What form would *you* choose if you had the choice?

The kids in the stories that follow have a chance to answer those questions—sometimes to their delight, sometimes to their utter terror.

So turn the page and come on in.

It's time to shape up!

HOMEWARD BOUND

by Bruce Coville

Jamie stood on the steps of his uncle's house and looked up. The place was tall and bleak. With its windows closed and shuttered, as they were now, it was easy to imagine the building was actually trying to keep him out.

"This isn't home," he thought rebelliously. "It's not home, and it never will be."

A pigeon fluttered onto the lawn nearby. Jamie started, then frowned. His father had raised homing pigeons, and the two of them had spent many happy hours together, tending his flock. But the sight of the bird now, with the loss of his father still so fresh in his mind, only stirred up memories he wasn't yet ready to deal with.

He looked at the house again and was struck by an odd feeling: while this wasn't home, coming here had somehow taken him one step closer to finding it. That feeling had to do with the horn, of course; of that much he was certain.

Jamie was seven the first time he had seen the horn hanging on the wall of his uncle's study.

"Narwhal," said his uncle, following the boy's gaze. "It's a whale with a horn growing out of the front of its head." He put one hand to his forehead and thrust out a finger to illustrate, as if Jamie were some sort of idiot.

"Sort of a seagoing unicorn," he continued. "Except, of course, that it's real instead of imaginary. I'd rather you didn't touch it. I paid dearly to get it."

Jamie had stepped back behind his father without speaking. He hadn't dared to say what was on his mind. Grown-ups, especially his uncle, didn't like to be told they were wrong.

But his uncle *was* wrong. The horn had not come from a narwhal, not come from the sea at all.

It was the horn of a genuine unicorn.

Jamie couldn't have explained how he knew this was so. But he did, as surely—and mysteriously—as his father's pigeons knew their way home. Thinking of that moment of certainty now, he was reminded of those stormy nights when he and his father had watched lightning crackle through the summer sky. For an instant, everything would be outlined in light. Then, just as quickly, the world would be plunged back into darkness, with nothing remaining but a dazzling memory.

That was how it had been with the horn, five years ago.

And now Jamie was twelve, and his father was dead, and he had been sent to live with this rich, remote man who had always frightened him so much.

Oddly, that fear didn't come from his uncle. Despite his stern manner, the man was always quiet and polite with Jamie. Rather, he had learned the fear from his father. The two men had not been together often, for his uncle frequently disappeared on mysterious "business trips" lasting weeks or even months on end. But as Jamie had watched his father grow nervous and unhappy whenever his brother was due to return, he came to sense that the one man had some strange hold over the other.

It frightened him.

Yet as scared as he was, as sad and lonely over the death of his father, one small corner of his soul was burning now with a fierce joy because he was finally going to be close to the horn.

Of course, in a way, he had never been apart from it. Ever since that first sight, five years ago, the horn had shimmered in his memory. It was the first thing he thought of when he woke up, and the last at night when he went to sleep. It was a gleaming beacon in his dreams, reassuring him no matter how cruel and ugly a day might have been, there was a reason to go on, a reason to be. His one glimpse of the horn had filled him with a sense of beauty and rightness so powerful it had carried him through these five years.

Even now, while his uncle was droning on about the household rules, he saw it again in that space in the back of his head where it seemed to reside. Like a shaft of never-ending light, it tapered through the darkness of his mind, wrist thick at its base, ice-pick sharp at its tip, a spiraled wonder of icy, pearly whiteness. And while Jamie's uncle was telling him the study was off-limits, Jamie was trying to figure out how quickly he could slip in there to see the horn again.

For once again his uncle was wrong. No place that held the horn could be off-limits to him. It was too deeply a part of him.

That was why he had come here so willingly, despite his fear of his uncle. Like the pigeons, he was making his way home.

Jamie listened to the big clock downstairs as it marked off the quarter hours. When the house had been quiet for seventy-five minutes he took the flashlight from under his pillow, climbed out of bed, and slipped on his robe. Walking softly, he made his way down the hall, enjoying the feel of the thick carpet like moss beneath his feet.

He paused at the door of the study. Despite his feelings, he hesitated. What would his uncle say, or do, if he woke and caught him here?

The truth was, it didn't matter. He had no choice. He had to see the horn again.

Turning the knob of the door, he held his breath against the inevitable click. But when it came, it was mercifully soft. He stepped inside and flicked on his flashlight.

His heart lurched as the beam struck the opposite wall and showed an empty place where the horn had once hung. A little cry slipped through his lips before he remembered how important it was to remain silent.

He swung the light around the room, and breathed a sigh of relief. The horn—the alicorn, as his reading had told him it was called—lay across his uncle's desk.

He stepped forward, almost unable to believe that the moment he had dreamed of all these years was finally at hand.

He took another step, and another.

He was beside the desk now, close enough to reach out and touch the horn.

And still he hesitated.

Part of that hesitation came from wonder, for the horn was even more beautiful than he had remembered. Another part of it came from a desire to make this moment last as long as he possibly could. It was something he had been living toward for five years now, and he wanted to savor it. But the biggest part of his hesitation came from fear. He had a sense that once he had touched the horn, his life might never be the same again.

That didn't mean he wouldn't do it.

But he needed to prepare himself. So for a while he simply stood in the darkness, gazing at the horn. Light seemed to play beneath its surface, as if there was something alive inside it—though how that could be after all this time he didn't know.

Finally he reached out to stroke the horn. Just stroke it. He wasn't ready, yet, to truly embrace whatever mystery was waiting for him. Just a hint, just a teasing glimpse, was all he wanted.

His fingertip grazed the horn and he cried out in terror as the room lights blazed on, and his uncle's powerful voice thundered over him, demanding to know what was going on.

Jamie collapsed beside the desk. His uncle scooped him up and carried him back to his room.

A fever set in, and it was three days before Jamie got out of bed again.

He had vague memories of people coming to see him during that time—of a doctor who took his pulse and temperature; of an older woman who hovered beside him, spooning a thin broth between his lips and wiping his forehead with a cool cloth; and most of all of his uncle, who loomed over his bed like a thundercloud, glowering down at him.

His only other memories were of the strange dream that gripped him over and over again, causing him to thrash and cry out in terror. In the dream he was running through a deep forest. Something was behind him, pursuing him. He leaped over mossy logs, splashed through cold streams, crashed through brambles and thickets. But no matter how he tried, he couldn't escape the fierce thing that was after him—a thing that wore his uncle's face.

More than once Jamie sat up in bed, gasping and covered with sweat. Then the old woman, or the doctor, would speak soothing words and try to calm his fears.

Once he woke quietly. He could hear doves cooing outside his window. Looking up, he saw his uncle standing beside the bed, staring down at him angrily.

Why? wondered Jamie. *Why doesn't he want me to touch the horn?*

But he was tired, and the question faded as he slipped back into his dreams.

He was sent away to a school, where he was vaguely miserable but functioned well enough to keep the faculty at a comfortable distance. The other students, not so easily escaped, took some delight in trying to torment the dreamy boy who was so oblivious to their little world of studies and games, their private wars and rages. After a while, they gave up; Jamie didn't react enough to make their tortures worth the effort on any but the most boring of days.

He had other things to think about, memories and mysteries that absorbed him and carried him through the year, aware of the world around him only enough to move from one place to another, to answer questions, to keep people away.

The memories had two sources. The first was the vision that had momentarily dazzled him when he touched the horn, a tantalizing instant of joy so deep and powerful it had shaken him to the roots of his being. Hints of green, of cool, of wind in his face and hair whispered at the edges of that vision.

He longed to experience it again.

The other memories echoed from his fever dreams, and were not so pleasant. They spoke only of fear, and some terrible loss he did not understand.

Christmas, when it finally came, was difficult. As the other boys were leaving for home his uncle sent word that urgent business would keep him out of town throughout the holiday. He paid the headmaster handsomely to keep an eye on Jamie and feed him Christmas dinner.

The boy spent a bleak holiday longing for his father. Until now his obsession with the horn had shielded him from the still-raw pain of that loss. But the sounds and smells of the holiday, the tinkling bells, the warm spices, the temporary but real goodwill surrounding him, all stirred the sorrow inside him, and he wept himself to sleep at night.

He dreamed. In his dreams his father would reach out to take his hand. "We're all lost," he would whisper, as he had the day he died. "Lost, and aching to find our name, so that we can finally go home again."

When Jamie woke, his pillow would be soaked with sweat, and tears.

The sorrow faded with the return of the other students, and the resumption of a daily routine. Even so, it was a relief when three months later his uncle sent word that Jamie would be allowed to come back for the spring holiday.

The man made a point of letting Jamie know he had hidden the horn by taking him into the study soon after the boy's arrival at the house. He watched closely as Jamie's eyes flickered over the walls, searching for the horn, and seemed satisfied at the expression of defeat that twisted his face before he closed in on himself, shutting out the world again.

But Jamie had become cunning. The defeat he showed his uncle was real. What the man didn't see, because the boy buried it as soon as he was aware of it, was that the defeat was temporary. For hiding the horn didn't make any difference. Now that Jamie had touched it, he was bound to it. Wherever it was hidden, he would find it. Its call was too powerful to mistake.

Even so, Jamie thought he might lose his mind before

he got the chance. Day after day his uncle stayed in the house, guarding his treasure. Finally, on the morning of the fifth day, an urgent message pulled him away. Even then the anger that burned in his face as he stormed through the great oak doors, an anger Jamie knew was rooted in being called from his vigil, might have frightened someone less determined.

The boy didn't care. He would make his way to the horn while he had the chance.

He knew where it was, of course—had known from the evening of the first day.

It was in his uncle's bedroom.

The room was locked. Moving cautiously, Jamie slipped downstairs to the servants' quarters and stole the master key, then scurried back to the door. To his surprise he felt no fear.

He decided it was because he had no choice; he was only doing what he had to do.

He twisted the key in the lock and swung the door open.

His uncle's room was large and richly decorated, filled with heavy, carefully carved furniture. Above the dresser hung a huge mirror.

Jamie hesitated for just a moment, then lay on his stomach and peered beneath the bed.

The horn was there, wrapped in a length of blue velvet.

He reached in and drew the package out. Then he stood and placed it gently on the bed. With reverent fingers he unrolled the velvet. Cradled by the rich blue fabric, the horn looked like a comet blazing across a midnight sky.

This time there could be no interruption. Hesitating for no more than a heartbeat, he reached out and clutched the horn with both hands.

He cried out in agony, and in awe. For a moment he thought he was going to die. The feelings the horn unleashed within him seemed too much for his body to hold. He didn't die, though his heart was racing faster than it had any right to.

"More," he thought, as images of the place he had seen in his dreams rushed through his mind. "I have to know more."

He drew the horn to his chest and laid his cheek against it.

He thought his heart would beat its way out of his body.

And it still wasn't enough.

He knew what he had to do next. But he was afraid.

Fear made no difference. He remembered again what his father had said about people aching to find their true name. He was close to his now. *No one can come this close and not reach out for the answer*, he thought. *The emptiness would kill them on the spot.*

And so he did what he had to do, fearful as it was. Placing the base of the horn against the foot of the massive bed, he set the tip of it against his heart.

Then he leaned forward.

The point of the horn pierced his flesh like a sword made of fire and ice. He cried out, first in pain, then in joy and wonder. Finally the answer was clear to him, and he understood his obsession, and his loneliness.

"No wonder I didn't fit," he thought, as his fingers fused, then split into cloven hooves.

The transformation was painful. But the joy so far surpassed it that he barely noticed the fire he felt as his neck began to stretch, and the horn erupted from his brow. "No wonder, no wonder—no, it's all wonder, wonder, wonder and joy!"

He reared back in triumph, his silken mane streaming behind him, as he trumpeted the joyful discovery that he was, and always had been, and always would be, a unicorn.

And knowing his name, he finally knew how to go home. Hunching the powerful muscles of his hind legs, he launched himself toward the dresser. His horn struck the mirror, and it shattered into a million pieces that crashed and tinkled into two different worlds.

He hardly noticed. He was through, and home at last.

No, said a voice at the back of his head. *You're not home yet*.

He stopped. It was true. He wasn't home yet, though he was much closer. But there was still more to do, and further to go.

How could that be? He knew he was, had always been, a unicorn. Then he trembled, as he realized his father's last words were still true. There was something inside that needed to be discovered, to be named.

He whickered nervously as he realized all he had

really done was come back to where most people begin—his own place, his own shape.

He looked around. He was standing at the edge of a clearing in an old oak wood. Sunlight filtered through the leaves, dappling patches of warmth onto his flanks. He paused for a moment, taking pleasure in feeling his own true shape at last.

Suddenly he shivered, then stood stock-still as the smell of the girl reached his nostrils.

The scent was sweet, and rich, and he could resist it no more than he had resisted the horn. He began trotting in her direction, sunlight bouncing off the horn that jutted out from his forehead.

He found her sitting beneath an apple tree, singing to herself while she brushed her honey-colored hair. Doves rustled and cooed at the edges of the clearing. They reminded him of the pigeons his father had raised.

As he stood and watched her, every fiber of his being cried out that there was danger here. But it was not in the nature of the unicorn to resist such a girl.

Lowering his head, he walked forward.

"So," she said. "You've come at last."

He knelt beside her, and she began to stroke his mane. Her fingers felt cool against his neck, and she sang to him in a voice that seemed to wash away old sorrows. He relaxed into a sweet silence, content for the first time that he could remember.

He wanted the moment to go on forever.

But it ended almost instantly as the girl slipped a

golden bridle over his head, and his uncle suddenly stepped into the clearing.

The man was wearing a wizard's garb, which didn't surprise Jamie. Ten armed soldiers stood behind him.

Jamie sprang to his feet. But he had been bound by the magic of the bridle; he could neither run, nor attack.

Flanks heaving, he stared at his wizard uncle.

"Did you really think you could get away from me?" asked the man.

I have! Jamie thought fiercely, knowing the thought would be understood.

"Don't be absurd!" snarled his uncle. "I'll take your horn, as I did your father's. And then I'll take your shape, and finally your memory. You'll come back with me and be no different than he was—a dreamy, foolish mortal, lost and out of place."

Why? thought Jamie. *Why would anyone want to hold a unicorn?*

His uncle didn't answer.

Jamie locked eyes with him, begging him to explain.

No answer came. But he realized he had found a way to survive. Just as the golden bridle held him helpless, so his gaze could hold his uncle. As long as he could stare into the man's eyes, he could keep him from moving.

He knew, too, that as soon as he flinched, the battle would be over.

Jamie had no idea how long the struggle actually lasted. They seemed to be in a place apart, far away

14

from the clearing, away from the girl and the soldiers.

He began to grow fearful. Sooner or later he would falter and his uncle would regain control. It wasn't enough to hold him. He had to conquer him.

But how? *How?*

He couldn't win unless he knew why he was fighting. He had to discover why his uncle wanted to capture and hold him.

But the only way to do that was to look deeper inside the man. The idea frightened him; he didn't know what he would find there. Even worse, it would work two ways. He couldn't look deeper into his uncle, without letting his uncle look more deeply into him.

He hesitated. But there was no other way. Accepting the risk, he opened himself to his uncle.

At the same time he plunged into the man's soul.

His uncle cried out, then dropped to his knees and buried his face in his hands, trembling with the humiliation of being seen.

Jamie trembled too, for the emptiness he found inside this man could swallow suns and devour planets. This was the hunger that had driven him to capture unicorns, in the hope that their glory could fill his darkness.

Then, at last, Jamie knew what he must do. Stepping forward, he pressed the tip of his horn against his uncle's heart.

He had been aware of his horn's healing power, of course. But this was the first time he had tried to use it. He wasn't expecting the shock of pain that jolted through him, or the wave of despair that followed as he took in the emptiness, and the fear and the hunger that had driven his uncle for so long.

He wanted to pull away, to run in terror.

But if he did, it would only start all over again. Only a healing would put an end to the pursuit. And this was the only way to heal this man, this wizard, who, he now understood, had never really been his uncle, but only his captor. He had to be seen, in all his sorrow and his ugliness; seen, and accepted, and loved. Only then could he be free of the emptiness that made him want to possess a unicorn.

Jamie trembled as the waves of emptiness and sorrow continued to wash through him. But at last he was nearly done. Still swaying from the effort, he whispered to the man: "Go back. Go back and find your name. And then—*go home.*"

That was when the sword fell, slicing through his neck.

It didn't matter, really, though he felt sorry for his "uncle," who began to weep, and sorrier still for the soldier who had done the deed. He knew it would be a decade or so before the man could sleep without mind-twisting nightmares of the day he had killed a unicorn.

But for Jamie himself, the change made no difference. Because he still was what he had always been, what he always would be, what a unicorn had simply been an appropriate shape to hold. He was a being of power and light.

He shook with delight as he realized that he had named himself at last.

He turned to the wizard, and was amazed. No longer hampered by mere eyes, he could see that the same thing was true for his enemy—as it was for the girl, as it was for the soldiers.

They were *all* beings of power and light.

The terrible thing was, they didn't know it.

Suddenly he understood. This was the secret, the unnamed thing his father had been trying to remember: that we are all beings of power and light. And all the pain, all the sorrow—it all came from not knowing this simple truth.

Why? wondered Jamie. *Why don't any of us know how beautiful we really are?*

And even that question became unimportant, because his father had come to take him home, and suddenly he wasn't just a unicorn, but was all unicorns, was part of every wise and daring being that had worn that shape and that name, every unicorn that had ever lived, or ever would live. And he felt himself stretch to fill the sky, as the stars came tumbling into his body, stars at his knees and at his hooves, at his shoulder and his tail, and most of all a shimmer of stars that lined the length of his horn, a horn that stretched across the sky, pointing out, for anyone who cared to look, the way to go home.

I Was a Bestselling Teenage Werewolf

by Lawrence Watt-Evans

Okay, so you've read my first book—everybody's read my first book, and if you haven't I'm sure you can find a copy somewhere. It's called *Moon Child* because my publisher's legal department insisted that I couldn't call it *I Was a Teenage Werewolf* on account of that old movie. You must have heard of the book—I mean, it did eleven weeks on *The New York Times* bestseller list, and it wasn't *that* long ago.

Anyway, *Moon Child* will give you the whole story about how I got to be a werewolf, and I swear, just as the book says, I thought it was a dog, and as far as I know it's still loose. The book tells you how I tore up the family next door, how I got arrested—I still can't believe that every single hair and drop of blood turned back to human like that, I mean, *really*, isn't that incredible? And it covers the trial, and all the fuss about the lawyers, and the multiple-personality plea, and the riot at the sentencing, and all that stuff.

And if you can't find the book, you probably read it all in the papers. So you know all that. And you know that I wrote the book in my cell during the trial, and then at the hospital afterward, and it got rushed into print because while lots of people have written about werewolves, this was the first book written by a real, live, court-certified werewolf.

So did you know that it sold 1.2 million copies, at $24.95 each? Sounds pretty good, right?

Well, it should have been, yeah, because even after my agent took his fifteen percent and all that, I socked away three million bucks, and I thought I was all set.

Except about a million went in taxes, and another million for all those lawyers; and then there were the psychiatrists and the civil suits by the victims' heirs. Not to mention the gypsy witch who finally came up with a cure.

So when I came out on the other side, and all the bills were paid and the lawsuits settled and I had waivers and quitclaims up to my neck, what I *didn't* have was any of the money—in fact, I still *owed* about a million and a half! And I wasn't hot news anymore, either, and I'd missed my shot at a college education, what with going straight from my junior year of high school into five years of litigation.

So I wrote another book, called *After the Fang*. I mean, what else had I ever made any money at, besides writing—mowing lawns?

Never heard of *After the Fang*, have you? It bombed. I mean, totally. Got a nice, fat advance that won't earn out until the twenty-seventh century, at the rate it's going.

It isn't fair, you know. People have gotten rich writing about recovering from a troubled childhood, from bad marriages. But *nobody* wanted to read the story of an *ex*-werewolf recovering from bankruptcy.

Heck, if I'd known that, I might've *stayed* a werewolf— three days a month in the federal pen isn't that terrible.

And I didn't know what I was doing anyway, when I was wolfed out, so it really wasn't a big deal.

But at the time I wanted out, and I got it. And there I was, a million bucks in debt and flipping burgers for the rent money.

After that—well, I just held on for a while while I thought everything over. Eventually I realized that writing was still the way to go, but that nobody wanted to read 280 pages of a loser feeling sorry for himself. I needed something else to write about. I mean, *Moon Child* had everything—blood, death, dramatic courtroom scenes, everything. Even the animal rights people got into it. But *After the Fang* . . . well, nobody cared about my tax audit.

I thought about trying fiction, maybe doing a novel based on my experiences, but I couldn't do it. Couldn't come up with a plot to save my life, except just rehashing *Moon Child* and pretending it was somebody else.

And I couldn't sell any other nonfiction—I mean, what credentials did I have? I don't even have a high school diploma—I can't afford the mail-order kind, and I was in jail when the rest of my class graduated.

What was left of it, anyway—I really do feel sorry for poor Marcy.

Anyway, getting back on track here, I did finally hit on something. I had to borrow every cent I could for traveling money, and it took me a year and a half to find what I was after, but I did it.

I haven't finished the book yet, but it should be easy, and I think it's a sure thing. My old publisher doesn't agree, and they won't touch it, not after the lousy sales they had on *After the Fang*.

So I'm shopping it around, and I brought it to you folks first, because this is the kind of house I feel can really do the story justice. It's all true, every word. It's first-person stuff, with plenty of blood and sex. It's a winner. If you're interested, give me call.

But please, remember, evenings only. Don't try calling during the day.

I call my new book *Confessions of a Vampire*.

MYSELF

by Mark A. Garland

I'd been talking to myself a lot. Which wasn't good, really. They say that's a sign you're going crazy. I couldn't say anything out loud. I didn't dare. Not with the beast always around somewhere, listening, waiting. I had to be careful what I allowed it to hear.

I told myself I wasn't scared, and that it wasn't too late, wasn't hopeless. After all, there wasn't anyone else to save me or the others—or my parents, if they were still alive. I did have a plan, and it was a good one. I just had to do everything exactly right.

"I'm not crazy," I told myself.

Of course, I could be wrong. . . .

The control consoles were all lit up when the ship's computer woke me. The spacecraft had just received one of those burst transmissions another ship can send when it's close by. I checked the readout. The second ship, the *Safari*, was less than twenty hours away. Lights began flashing everywhere as the computer automatically downloaded and transmitted telemetry and flight systems data. It was pretty exciting.

The beast was excited, too. I could tell.

I didn't know how to transmit a voice message back, so I tried using the keyboard, typing the words in as if I were using my computer at home, or the terminal in my cabin on board. That's all there is to do on a ship like this. You sit at the screen and play computer games, or read books from the ship's diskette library. Or, when they'll let you, you run some of the programmable simulations stored in the ship's computer—everything from docking to landing to mission abort procedures.

I selected the communications program and it came right up. Luckily, the *Safari*'s ID codes were in the menu. I punched ENTER, and waited for the connection.

I thought about my father. "The beast wants to use our spacecraft to travel back to Earth," he had told me. My mother called it a hobgoblin, but she never saw it. She didn't know what to believe, and I didn't either, not at first. She thought it was all part of our being so far out in space, so alone; or some side effect of being asleep for so long during the journey from Earth to Jupiter; or some force Jupiter itself was emitting. But whatever it was, it was making Dad crazy.

"We have to be careful," Mom said, "or it will make *us* crazy, too."

"I'm not crazy," I told her.

"I don't think I am, either," she said. "But neither does your father."

I think my father was right, though. The beast is real, and I believe it will stop at nothing to find a way to leave Jupiter. In fact, I was counting on it.

"Greetings," someone on the *Safari* sent back. "Go ahead."

I did my best. My hands were shaking, so I kept missing letters on the keyboard. Slowly, though, I told the *Safari* I was the captain's son, that our ship, the *Venture*, had been disabled, and that the long-range antenna had been torn off, which was why we hadn't been communicating with Earth.

Then I waited.

Dad thought the beast was from Europa, Jupiter's very large, frozen moon. That was the part I still *don't* believe. That hobgoblin just seemed a little too familiar to me . . .

"I'm going to tell them everything!" I yelled at the beast. Not that saying so would change the hobgoblin's mind. It wants to feed on people—billions of people. It doesn't want to eat their bodies. It wants some part of their minds, their spirits; it wants to gnaw at who and what you are.

Not that it can read minds or anything, but it can read moods very well, and fear is one of its favorites. That's why I was trying so hard not to seem scared, and why I hadn't had any sleep in days. I knew that if I stayed in the ship's control room, and kept my mind occupied, and pretended I wasn't afraid, the beast would mostly stay away.

Not far away, though. It was always lurking somewhere in the ship's storage holds or the silent, empty crew quarters—or in the dining room, which was why I hadn't eaten much in days, either. A lot of the ship's lighting wasn't turned on, and I didn't know how to reprogram it. The first time I tried walking through the ship's darkened, lifeless corridors I started to feel like I couldn't breathe, and I felt the beast. I ran back to the control room, and stayed there.

28

But it knew enough to wait. And when I fell asleep, it came.

You can tell when the hobgoblin is close. It gives off a bone-shivering feeling. But it's worse when the beast touches you, feeding on some part of your insides that you can't get at, can't pull it off of. As long as it feeds there is nothing you can do to stop it, no way to escape. Until you wake up feeling like you haven't eaten or slept or had a drink of water in days. The feeling lasts for hours.

But that's when the beast seems the most . . . familiar.

I wasn't nearly enough food for it, not once it had gotten a taste, not once it knew the truth. It figured out what had happened, I'm sure of that, and what could happen, if it didn't remain stuck there, endlessly orbit-ing Jupiter—me living off the ship's recycling systems and food stores, the hobgoblin living off of me, until one of us ran out of food. . . .

"We want to speak to the captain," the message came back, more bright words appearing on one of the control room's console screens. They couldn't, of course.

I started typing again. "The captain thought he saw a monster. He thought it came aboard with him in the shuttle pod after he went down to Europa to take some samples. He thought the monster was going to take control of the ship and prevent us from establishing a colony, maybe even take the ship back to Earth. So he smashed the antenna, and jettisoned all the fuel."

I didn't want to tell them the rest, but I told myself I had to. I stuffed my fingers under my legs for a minute, to stop the shaking, but it didn't seem to help.

"After that," I typed, "we found out the rest of the crew was dead. Something went wrong with their sleep pods. We think that was the beast, though, not my dad. It was trying to wake the others up."

I sat for a long time, just watching the screen. There were dozens of people on the *Safari*, a whole community of families ready to start new lives on new worlds. But as close as they were, I had never been so alone in all my life.

Alone, except for that hobgoblin.

I've felt the beast before, like the time I was in my uncle's basement alone and someone turned off the lights, and I couldn't find my way out. Or the time I tried looking in the windows of the big, abandoned furnace factory near the edge of our hometown. And especially the time we went camping in the woods, and I got lost.

I remember stumbling around in the dark, wondering what was sneaking up on me, out there behind the trees. A ghastly thing, grinning inside, moving when I moved. I knew it was there. I just knew. A creature that never comes out in the daytime, never shows itself fully to the world. A foul, immortal thing that is simply going to get you, one way or another, before the night is through.

I caught a glimpse of the beast in the starlight that night. It was huge, all flat black, big at its shoulders and thick necked, with pointed ears like a wolf, and yellow-orange eyes that smoldered in the darkness. It had no face otherwise, no features at all. It had long, sinuous arms but no legs. Its great, bearlike shape seemed to taper near the ground, then come toward me, fading as it got close.

They cling to people, I think, like parasites. Some people see them under their beds, in their closets, or in the attic of a haunted house. But the beast in the woods was bigger. The one on the ship was bigger still.

That hobgoblin knew I'd seen it that night. I think that's what kept it away. But it doesn't care now. Somehow, out here, it has become a completely separate entity. It isn't just a form, it has substance. It exists. It's as real as I am.

Unlike Dad, I don't believe the hobgoblin came from Europa. I think we brought it with us from Earth, inside us, and it's managed to set itself free.

"Where is the captain now?" the *Safari* finally asked.

"He's down on Europa again, with my mom. They might still be alive. He went back to see if he could learn more about the beast, maybe some way to fight it. Or he thought it would go back down there with him, I'm not sure. My mom was still saying he had gone crazy. She gave me something to make me sleep, then she took the second pod and went after him. After a while, I woke up. They haven't come back."

"You are the only one on board?" the voice from the *Safari* asked.

I wanted to answer. I tried to hold one hand still with the other, so I could type one-fingered, but the shaking had just gotten too bad. The *Safari*'s crew didn't type anything else for a while, either.

31

"Won't be long!" I yelled, sitting on my hands again. "I'm finally going home! I'm going to leave you here to rot!" I knew what it wanted. I knew it was listening to every word.

The next message from the *Safari* showed up on a different screen, which meant that they were sending it to Earth. It read, "The captain's son seems to be the only survivor, and he sounds like he is out of his mind. He may have killed the entire crew somehow. We're planning a rescue mission to Europa. Meanwhile, we're going in."

That hobgoblin wanted to be rescued even more than I did. "I'll send you back a postcard!" I yelled. It didn't think I knew its plan. Which was all part of my plan. I decided to try and get some rest.

The control consoles were lit up again when the computer woke me, just the way I had programmed it to. I typed in a new command, then checked the time.

"A few minutes to go, and the *Safari* will be docking!" I shouted. According to the screen, they had been trying to contact me again. There were several messages. I decided none of them were important just now. The *Safari*'s crew didn't know. They didn't believe. And anyway, it didn't matter.

I only had one chance to beat that hobgoblin, and possibly save myself, and my parents. And the less the *Safari* knew about it, the better . . .

Suddenly, I felt the fear getting hold of me once more. It was the beast, and it was partly because I was thinking about my mother and father again. I felt like I wanted to cry, right then and there.

The beast was coming near, moving through the empty corridors, approaching the control room, touching the door, opening it like you or I. It was so hungry with anticipation, so full of craving. Drooling, I think. I knew that if I turned away from the consoles it would be there, just standing there in plain sight, looking over my shoulder, reading the words on the screen. It's not a stealthy monster like they are on Earth. It's not afraid of the light anymore. It's not afraid of anything.

It made me feel cold inside as it listened and watched. But I had to make it think I wasn't afraid either, or it might have figured out my plan. Had to concentrate on the control consoles. Besides, you don't want to look into those glowing eyes.

Fight it, I said to myself. I took a deep breath.

The status board lit up. Ready for docking. I logged on. "Use the cargo hatch," I typed. "The regular hatch doesn't work anymore. We . . . I will see you there."

The cargo hatch is big. Very big. I didn't want anything to get in the way.

I sensed the hobgoblin leave, headed for the main cargo bay, of course. It was time for me to go, too.

My legs were shaking now, but I made them carry me through the ship, until I arrived on the upper level in the loading bay's glassed-in control and observation station. It's like having a balcony seat for a stage show, and it's completely sealed from the bay itself.

Loud clicks and booms echoed through the whole ship,

all coming from the PA system, the sounds of one hull bumping another, of hatch couplings clamping down.

Hobgoblins, I was guessing, are only just so smart. . . .

I could see it there below me in the cavernous cargo hold, right in front of the big airlock door, not taking any chances, and not the least bit interested in me anymore. It held there, waiting, bigger than a pickup truck, dull black and almost out of focus, so details were still hard to see. The beast seemed to absorb much of the light that touched it. Its arms clung to the bulkheads. And it had legs.

The red STAND BY light flashed over the door. Then another, yellow light, indicating a positive ship-to-ship seal. The monster crouched to one side of the hatch as the final green GO light blinked on.

The hatch door slid aside and the hobgoblin made its charge—a fierce, flying leap that sent it though the opening with a speed beyond the knowledge of human eyes. I'd always known they could do that. Always.

But this time, his form and substance buoyed by the tremendous outward rush of air leaving the cargo bay, the hobgoblin went even faster than normal. Faster than the beast itself could imagine. And in my mind, I swear even in my ears, I could hear the monster's furious, horrified scream as it realized it had flung itself out into the cold, empty vacuum of space around Jupiter.

As it realized (too late, of course) that there was no ship there for it to enter. Before it could turn around, the hatch had already closed.

*   *   *

Myself

I made my way back to the main console in the control room, sat down at the keyboard, and canceled the rescue simulation. Then I checked on the messages the *Safari* had sent back when I'd been sleeping. The most recent message said they'd be docking in fifty-seven minutes.

I logged on, and told them to come ahead, told them I was okay and I'd be waiting, quietly.

"I'm not crazy," I told myself. "I'm not scared."

The *Safari* sent another message, saying everything would be okay.

I told them not to look out any of the windows.

FROG PRINCES

by Janni Lee Simner

Kim found her frog in the swamp, while wading through ankle-deep mud with her brother and sister.

"It's ugly," Kevin said.

"It is not," Kim insisted, though she knew he was right. It was more brown than green, with patches of skin peeling off, lumps all over, and one eye higher than the other. She'd picked it because of the eyes, though. When she looked at them, the frog looked back, and its eyes weren't blank and empty like most frog eyes. She didn't tell Kevin, though. Or Alicia.

"It's *gross*," her sister said. But she said that about every frog she saw.

"Of course it's not handsome," Kim's mother said when they returned home. "Frogs with princes in them never are."

Kim hadn't thought of that, but it made sense, so she smiled at Kevin and Alicia as if she'd known all along.

"Oh, yuck." Alicia frowned as she washed the mud off her shoes. Mud coated Kim's shoes, too, but she didn't care so much. "That means you've got to kiss it, you know."

"Big deal," Kevin said. "I'd rather kiss a frog than a girl." Puckering his lips, he leaned toward the shoebox in Kim's hands.

38

Kim yanked the box away. "You leave my frog alone!"

"You really think there *is* a prince in there, don't you?" Kevin teased.

"I do not," Kim said. But pulling the shoebox close to her chest, she turned and ran to her room.

Kim set the shoebox down on the floor. Lifting the cover, she looked at the frog. It stared back with big, round eyes. Somehow, unlike Kim, the frog wasn't muddy at all.

Kim reached in and touched it. It felt strange— smooth and velvety, nothing like the slimy swamp she'd pulled it from. The frog kept staring as she ran her hand along its lumpy back.

She liked the frog, lumps and patches and all. But she'd never met a prince, outside of books and cartoons.

Kim picked up the frog with one hand. It didn't try to jump away, not even when she set it down on her desk.

Making sure the door was closed, she leaned forward. She shut her eyes, scrunched up her face, and kissed the frog, very quickly, right on the lips.

A crash sent her sprawling backward. When she opened her eyes, her desk lay in pieces on the floor. In the middle of the pieces sprawled a man, rubbing his head.

He didn't look like anything from a book or cartoon. He looked more like the pictures of TV stars Alicia had on her walls—tall and blond, with cold, blue eyes. Only he was dressed funnier than in Alicia's pictures, with a blue velvet cloak, pants that only reached his knees, and pointy shoes. A shiny gold band circled his head. He brushed the dust from his clothes and looked around the room.

"Where is she?" he demanded. His voice was rich and deep, much more so than any of the TV stars'.

"Where is who?" Kim stared at the prince. She'd like him more if he smiled. Frogs never smiled either, but that was because they were frogs.

"The beautiful lady who set me free," the prince said.

"Oh." Kim shoved her hands into her pockets. "That's me."

The man slowly stood. He looked down at her, and something about his hard gaze made Kim suddenly aware of the splatters of mud that still clung to her face and bare arms, of the way she smelled faintly of swamp water.

"You're hardly a proper princess," he said.

"I'm not a princess at all. We don't have princesses here." Kim's class had talked about that in school just last week. "It's because of the Revolutionary War," she explained.

The man stroked his chin thoughtfully. "Well, there *is* some precedent for a prince marrying a peasant. Perhaps you have secret royal blood, or a magical talent no one knows about yet."

"I'm not a peasant." Kim wondered if she ought to

be offended. "We don't have those here, either." She thought that was also because of the Revolutionary War, but wasn't sure.

The prince ignored her and kept talking, as if to himself. "We could clean you up, get you into a decent dress, uncover your hidden beauty. Yes, I think that would work quite well, indeed."

"I hate dresses," Kim said. It was too easy to catch them in doorways, or trip and tear them. But the prince ignored that, too. Instead he nodded, once, as if he'd made a decision. He held out his hand to her.

"Would you do me the honor," he asked, his voice deeper than ever, "of taking my hand in marriage?"

"No way," Kim told him.

"W-what?" The prince stammered slightly, and his face crinkled into a rather unprincely expression.

"I said I'm not a peasant, I'm not going to wear a dress, and I'm definitely not going to marry you!"

"B-but," the prince stammered again, "this is unprecedented! What—what would your father say?"

"Dad and Mom would both say to come back after I graduate college." They'd said just that last week, to a boy who'd come by to see Alicia. Alicia had been furious. "*I'd* say—"

But the prince never let Kim tell him what she thought. His face turned red with anger. But instead of yelling, he whirled around and stormed from the room. Kim listened as his footsteps retreated down the stairs. Then she turned back to her splintered desk, searching for the shoebox.

The torn cardboard still smelled of swamp water, but of course the frog was gone.

Kim found another shoebox in Alicia's closet—Alicia had lots of shoes—and she went back to the swamp. This time, Kim didn't let Kevin or Alicia go with her.

As soon as Kim returned home, Alicia peeked into the box. "Oh, gross. This one's uglier than the first one."

"I'll bet you're gonna tell us there's a prince in it, too," Kevin taunted.

"Am not," Kim said. She brushed past them up the stairs, ignoring the muddy water that dripped from her jeans and T-shirt. She set the shoebox down on her dresser and lifted the cover. The frog stared out at her, with bulging eyes that weren't blank and empty like most frog eyes. Kim smiled and set the cover down again.

Of course there was a prince inside. No way would she kiss him, though. She'd met frogs before, and she'd met a prince, too.

This time, she was keeping the frog.

TRICKY COYOTE

by Susan J. Kroupa

Jimmy Shupla never wanted to be anything other than human. He especially didn't want to be a coyote. In all the Hopi stories his grandmother told him, coyotes were the silliest of animals—always trying to trick others and always having their tricks backfire. Still, the day he turned into a coyote he wasn't entirely surprised. Coyotes had always haunted the edges of his life.

Hadn't his grandmother told him she'd spotted a coyote on the day of his naming when he was just a baby? And three years ago, when he was eight, he'd seen one at his initiation. It trotted right through the center of the village, past the old stone houses and the kiva, and then calmly loped off. Everyone who saw it laughed. Silly Coyote was up to his tricks again.

"Maybe Coyote came because he is your animal guide," his grandmother said that day.

"How is he going to help me?" Jimmy asked. "Everyone always laughs at Coyote." He wished that Badger or Eagle had appeared at his initiation instead.

His grandmother frowned. "If you can learn from him, that is what matters. Worrying too much about what other people think can be a pathway to becoming a witch."

Jimmy didn't want to be a witch, using power to

hurt others, but he secretly hoped that his grandmother was wrong about Coyote being his animal guide.

Then, to his dismay, a coyote appeared again, this time when his mother showed up at his grandmother's house and said she was taking Jimmy to live with her in Apache Junction. She said she finally had a decent job and a trailer with enough space for two. Everyone was surprised by this. She had always said it was hard enough for one person to live on what she earned waiting tables in Apache Junction. She had always said there were no jobs on the reservation. But his grandmother once told Jimmy that his mother preferred the Anglo cities to the Hopi villages.

"She doesn't hold much to the old ways," his grandmother said, disapproval deepening the lines on her face.

Still, his grandmother and grandfather had let his mother take him away. All the way out to the car he had waited for them to call out, to tell her to stop, but they hadn't. He saw the coyote out the car window as he rode beside his mother down the mesa. He was sure he saw it because his eyes stayed dry and clear even though his chest cramped so tight he could hardly breathe.

"We have TV and you'll have your own room," his mother said. "And running water."

He wondered why that was better than having his grandparents sleeping beside him.

It took hours to drive to Apache Junction, a desert town near Phoenix. His mother took him to a small trailer that sweltered on a patch of dirt near dozens of other trailers. The walls shook with every gust of wind, and Jimmy missed his grandmother's solid stone house, which had shut out the weather for centuries.

The next morning, as he walked down the long gravel road to the bus stop, he saw a coyote. It crossed in front of him, but then stopped and looked him in the eye, something not even a friendly dog would normally do. It stared at him, its face sad.

"Go away!" Jimmy said, shaken. "I don't want you around." The coyote turned then, and loped off.

At school that day he discovered that—despite its name—Apache Junction had hardly any Indian kids. Some of the boys in the class laughed out loud when the teacher announced that Jimmy had come from the Hopi reservation. The teacher glared at them, but they still snickered in loud whispers. During the first recess, he met a Navajo boy named Delbert, and sat with him at lunch. They shot hoops together during the second recess, too, until they suddenly were surrounded by the other boys from the class. A dark, stocky boy grabbed the ball.

"Hey, Miguel, give it back!" Delbert shouted.

Miguel just laughed and threw it to one of his friends. They tossed it back and forth.

Jimmy jumped after it but missed, and Miguel grabbed his shirt, holding his fist so it almost touched Jimmy's nose. He was a good head taller than either

Jimmy or Delbert, and Jimmy thought he looked more Indian than Hispanic, but then Miguel's words drove all such thoughts out of his head.

"You want it? You want it? I'll give it to you!" Miguel's black eyes held nothing but hatred.

Jimmy stared at Miguel's shirt, frozen, not even daring to breathe. Finally Miguel released him and turned away, and the boys all left, taking the ball with them. Jimmy and Delbert walked back to the classroom then, Jimmy forcing his eyes to stay dry even though his whole body shook with anger.

After that, he and Delbert stuck close to the playground teacher during recess.

But the teacher couldn't protect him after he got off the bus. The worst discovery of Jimmy's first day at school was that Miguel lived in the same trailer park. He and his friend Nick, a skinny kid with stringy blond hair, poked and shouted at Jimmy the entire walk home. After a few days, they began chasing him down the gravel road, punching him if he didn't run fast enough to escape them.

It was one of those times that it happened. He was walking home from the bus stop, suffocating in the brutal September heat, listening to the footsteps behind him. Miguel and Nick, as usual. Jimmy wished they'd leave him alone, wished he were strong enough to beat them up. He hated them. Stupid bullies who made his life miserable. An anger rose within him, churning like a dust devil. It swirled inside until he felt he was going to split apart, and then he was dizzy as if it had moved outside him and sucked him up. The ground seemed to spring toward him.

One of the boys yelled, but Jimmy hardly heard it. An overpowering *stench* filled his nose. Worse, when he looked down at himself he saw four legs. Four furry legs. He turned his head and saw a long gray-brown back that ended in a tail. *A coyote,* he thought in dismay, but there was no time to consider how this had come about.

Already the stench began to sort itself into individual smells. The scent of Nick and Miguel jolted him with fear.

Humans! something deep inside him said. *Run!*

But the Jimmy part of him remembered the bruises he'd gotten from their punches. Remembered how humiliating it was to sit by the teacher during recess. The anger escaped his mouth in a snarl, and the sound reminded him that coyotes have sharp teeth.

He attacked Nick first, sinking his jaws into a piece of arm, smelling the blood as his teeth ripped through flesh. It made him sick and elated at the same time. Nick fell to the ground screaming. Miguel turned and ran back toward the bus stop. Jimmy caught up to him easily, surprised at how fast having four legs made him. He lunged at Miguel, tearing through his jeans but only grazing the skin.

He snapped again, but the voice within him was shouting, *No! Humans! Run! Run!* The fear rose from his very bones and he could ignore it no longer. He swerved around Miguel and bounded off into the desert, running, running, running, until heat and exhaustion overcame him. He slowed to a trot. *Hide!* said the voice inside.

Finally, he came upon an old paved road. He followed it until it crossed a wash. A culvert ran beneath the road. He crawled into it, into the cool dark, and lay there panting. Somewhere, in the back part of his mind, Jimmy wondered how he had become a coyote. But he was too tired to think about it. And then he fell asleep.

When he awoke, he was human again. He was lying in the culvert, clothed just as he'd been when he got off the bus, backpack and everything.

Maybe somehow he'd dreamed it all, but it felt too real for that. Maybe he was going crazy. How many times had his grandmother told him it was not the Hopi way to let oneself become angry? And to attack someone—his grandmother would call *that* crazy.

It was almost dark. He crawled out of the culvert and began walking down the road, wondering how he would ever find his way home. But before he'd gone very far, a police car came by and stopped beside him. A woman in a uniform rolled down the window.

"Jimmy Shupla?" she asked She had tired eyes like his mother's when she got off work.

Jimmy nodded, his heart pounding. Maybe they were going to arrest him for attacking those boys.

Instead, she smiled, and her eyes seemed less tired. She got out of the car. "A whole bunch of people are looking for you! Were you bitten by the coyote?"

Jimmy shook his head. *So it wasn't a dream,* he thought, his heart sinking.

"Well, that's a relief. Probably has rabies, attacking people like that. Let's get you home. Your mother's worried sick."

When they reached the trailer, Jimmy's mother rushed out to meet them, her eyes red and swollen from crying. She surprised him by how fiercely she hugged him. Later, he learned that Nick and Miguel were going to have to get shots in case the coyote had rabies. There was a big story about it on TV with pictures of people with rifles, and talk about a reward for the coyote's dead body.

That night, Jimmy lay in his room wishing his grandmother's walls of stone surrounded him. In spite of the heat, he shivered. Why did he have to have coyotes in his life anyway?

He pulled his pillow around his face. What if he turned into a coyote again and got killed? And what about the coyote with the sad face he'd seen on the first day of school? He hoped it was far away, safe from all the hunters' bullets. He pictured the coyote in his mind. *Stay away!* he told it. *Hide!*

And then something deep inside him began to tremble. How could his grandmother have let him leave? Why hadn't she kept him on the mesa where he belonged? What if the coyote with the sad eyes died? It would be his fault if it got shot. His eyes watered and he choked back the tears, but it was a long time that night before he finally fell asleep.

Nick and Miguel were at school the next day. Nick wore a big bandage on his arm. At recess, most of the class crowded around him to hear about the coyote. Jimmy and Delbert stood at the back of the group, listening.

"We were just walking home from the bus and *bap!* It sprang out of the bushes and attacked us," Nick said. Face flushed, eyes bright, he was plainly enjoying the attention. He brushed a strand of greasy blond hair off his face, then held his hand up to his chest. "Biggest coyote I've ever seen. More like a wolf. Right?" He looked at Miguel for confirmation, but Miguel stared at his feet as if he were afraid.

"And teeth!" Nick pointed to his bandage. "I got thirty-four stitches!"

Jimmy remembered the taste of flesh in his mouth and felt sick. He hoped his grandmother never found out.

On the way back into the classroom, Jimmy and Delbert ended up in line behind Miguel.

"That coyote didn't come out of the bushes," Miguel said in a low voice to another boy. "That boy—he changed into a coyote, like *that!*" He snapped his fingers. "Right before my eyes!" He turned then, and saw Jimmy. His eyes widened.

"I *saw* it!" Miguel's voice, defiant at first, trailed to a whisper. *"Brujo!"* He crowded forward into the line.

Jimmy found Delbert staring at him.

"He called you a *witch!*" Delbert said. "What does he mean?"

The words were out of Jimmy's mouth before he could think. "It just happened. I don't know how. I didn't *try* to be a coyote. . . . I didn't want to . . ."

But Delbert backed away from him, a look of horror on his face.

"Witch?" asked a thin, freckled girl beside Jimmy. She gave a loud cackle and chanted, "Witch, witch, where's your broomstick?"

"No, you gotta make it rhyme," Nick said, further up the line. "Witch, witch, you're a—" The bell rang, cutting him off, and then the teacher led them into class.

But Jimmy knew what Miguel and Delbert had meant. In Indian culture, witches weren't old women with black hats and broomsticks. They were people who used magic to hurt others. Sometimes witches made people sick. Sometimes they took the shape of animals. But they always used their magic for evil.

The rest of the day was awful. Jimmy wanted to tell Delbert he wasn't a witch. He didn't want to hurt anyone. But the bandage on Nick's arm made him wonder if he was lying to himself.

The awful day stretched into an awful week. Without Delbert to talk to at lunch and recess, school seemed endless. Nick and Miguel no longer bothered him on the walk home from the bus stop, but the way they watched him, as if he were a monster, made Jimmy almost wish they'd go back to chasing him. Even worse were the reports on the nightly news: on the weekend, volunteers from all over the state were going to help search for the coyote. Jimmy lay in bed at night and worried about the sad-faced coyote.

"Hide," he said silently, hoping it could hear. "And tell all your friends. Keep away from here."

The hunters arrived on Friday. As he walked home

from the bus stop, Jimmy saw the trucks clustered in the trailer park. The men held a big meeting and then got into their trucks and took off in giant clouds of dust.

At first, Jimmy huddled in the trailer, miserably waiting to hear a rifle shot. If a coyote died it'd be his fault. He thought about Delbert, who was afraid to even come near him now. And Miguel. Were they right? Was he a witch? If so, maybe he'd be better off dead. Maybe he ought to turn back into a coyote. Maybe he ought to let the hunters shoot *him*, instead of some innocent coyote who'd never attacked a human, who'd never sunk his teeth into flesh just because he was angry.

The longer he considered it, the more it seemed that changing back to a coyote was the right thing to do. Even if just thinking about it made him shake inside. The only problem was that he didn't know *how.* Could he change just by wanting to?

He waited until dusk and then walked outside in front of his trailer. He closed his eyes. *Coyote, coyote, coyote.* Shutting everything else out of his mind, he willed his body to comply. *Coyote, coyote, coyote.* He pictured himself as a coyote and directed all his energies to the picture. *Coyote, coyote, coyote.*

After a long time, when he became too tired to continue, he opened his eyes. His body was unchanged. But something moved in front of him. It was nearly dark and it took him a moment to see it. A coyote sat a few feet away, staring at him with the same sad look he'd seen before.

No! This wasn't what he wanted. Not here where the hunters would find it.

"Run!" he whispered. "Hide!"

The coyote stared back, but it was if Jimmy heard him say, *Don't worry. I'll be okay.* And the confidence behind the thought was great enough that Jimmy's fear for the coyote vanished, leaving room for other fears.

"I don't want to be a witch," Jimmy said, still in a whisper. "Don't make me a witch." Tears welled up unbidden in his eyes.

And again the coyote's thoughts came into his mind. *No one can make you a witch. Only you can do that.* And Jimmy remembered it wasn't the coyote part of him that had wanted to attack the boys.

The coyote trotted over to a trash can in front of a neighbor's trailer. Deftly, he jumped up on two legs and leaned over the top of the can, biting through the bag inside and fishing out something, which he ate. And then he disappeared into the night.

Jimmy was still standing in front of the trailer when his mother drove up a few minutes later.

"You need to come inside," she said. "I don't want you getting lost again." The fear in her voice was real. He remembered how she'd cried and hugged him when the policewoman had brought him home. Something in her eyes now reminded him of his grandmother.

"It's not safe out there until they catch that coyote," she said.

"That coyote won't hurt anyone again." The confidence in his voice brought a puzzled expression to his mother's face.

That night, Jimmy went to bed without bothering to watch the news. Coyote had said he'd be okay and Jimmy believed him. For the first time, he thought that maybe having Coyote as an animal guide wasn't so bad. Coyote, once with an endless desert to roam and hunt, now had to find food in garbage cans. The king of tricksters had pulled off the greatest trick of all: his whole world had changed and he'd survived.

Quite a trick, thought Jimmy. And he thought that maybe he could do the same.

SWAN SISTER

by Anne Mazer

Each night my seven brothers change into swans and fly out the doors, the windows, the chimney. The air is thick with feathers and dust. After my brothers have flown over the yard and out of sight, I, their younger sister, creep out of the house to pick up the feathers that lie on the dark grass like glowing swords.

The house is silent after they have left, and I go up to my room, where I pull the covers tightly around me. I lie awake, straining to hear the long, high calls that come through the window more and more faintly. When at last they cease, I fall asleep, though my nights are restless and troubled by dreams.

As a small child I stood on a dark lawn as seven white swans alighted in a circle around me. I held out pieces of crumbled bread, which they plucked delicately from my infant hand. It was just before dawn, and I had come out of bed early to see them. Then the swans rose in the air and disappeared into a small woods nearby. "Swans, come back!" I cried. "Swans, come back!"

Soon my seven brothers came out of the woods. They picked me up on their shoulders and threw me into the air, pretending to make me fly.

"Swans!" I sobbed.

My brothers bounced balls, gave me candy, showed

me books. But I refused to be consoled, and cried straight through to the night—when seven swans appeared in our living room and beat at the doors and windows until I let them out.

When I was a little older and understood that my brothers were the swans and the swans my brothers, I wanted to join them.

One evening when they came home from work, I ladled out the soup and heated the coffee. My brothers sat slumped at the table, not saying much, only glancing anxiously at the sky. Sometimes they dozed between spoonfuls of soup, and then I tapped them on the shoulders until they jerked awake.

When they were done eating they rose and went to the living room. I followed, asking questions. "Do you sleep in the air?"

My eldest brother looked out the window, and his eyes seemed to brighten. "Never."

"Are you scared of falling?" I asked my second brother.

Sometimes as I lay in bed at night, I imagined them falling to earth—the great wings collapsing, bright eyes closing—and animals of the forest finding them and tearing their flesh. I saw them caught in trees, hung on wires. Then I woke with a gasp and a cry and could not sleep again for hours.

My brother laughed. "Why scared? Swans don't fall. And even if I falter, the others will catch me. But it has never happened."

"What is it like?" I asked.

My brothers gazed out the windows, checked their watches, stroked their arms impatiently.

"What is what like?" my second brother said.

"The change . . . you know."

He whirled around, turned his back to me, as if protecting something I could not see.

My other brothers smiled at me and shook their heads. My eldest brother patted me on the back.

"Won't you tell me what it's like?" I pleaded.

The sun plummeted suddenly downward. It grew dark. My brothers stood motionless, scarcely breathing. Then their sturdy limbs, their strong legs and arms, dwindled into nothing and re-formed—from a breath of air—into large wings, sharp beaks, and downy feathers. It seemed then that they wanted to speak to me, to answer my question, but only strange, high-pitched cries issued from their throats as they burst free, flying through the doors and windows into the night sky.

I began to practice jumping, at first from our porch, then from the low branches of a tree. I spread out my arms, closed my eyes tightly, and imagined myself soaring. Yet, time after time, I fell straight to the ground, twisting ankles and bruising my legs.

My brothers looked after me, worried.

"Where did you get those bruises?"

"I fell. It was nothing."

"From where?"

"Out of the tree."

"The tree! What were you doing there?"

"Trying to fly."

My brothers frowned. "You'll only hurt yourself that way."

"Then show me how."

My eldest brother stroked his arms as if they were covered with invisible feathers. "We can't."

"Why not?"

They exchanged glances.

"Why won't you tell me!" I cried. "Why do you keep secrets from me?"

"It's not that," my seventh brother said. He touched my shoulder.

"We'd like to help you," said my second brother. "But we just don't know how."

"You have to find the way for yourself," my oldest brother said. "We did. . . ."

I searched their rooms for answers to my questions. I opened drawers, looked under piles of neatly folded socks, checked beds and mattresses. I felt along windows, lifted rugs, tapped the spines of old schoolbooks. I never found a trace of what I hoped for: a recipe, a message, a clue—even a single word written on a slip of paper, a word that would give me wings.

Then I began to go to the woods behind our house. I gathered leaves, roots, and twigs and crushed them between stones, mixed them with oil, and spread the often foul-smelling mess over my arms, legs, and face. In the morning I examined myself, hoping to see the first downy feathers or perhaps the beginning of a beak.

I bathed in ice-cold water, drank cups of vile-tasting tea.

I arranged swan feathers in intricate patterns and mumbled words over them during different phases of the moon.

Still, each night my brothers left me. They changed into swans. Their wings beat wildly against the walls. The house could not contain their fury and desire. I, too, reached out my arms—held them wide—as if I might also fly. My arms ached and strained, stretched almost out of their sockets.

"Take me with you!" I cried. "I can fly. I can!"

The swan cries of my brothers grew more and more urgent. Their beaks slashed against windows and curtains; their wings dashed against walls, overturning lamps, knocking down pictures.

My arms fell to my sides. I ran to the windows, flung open the doors. And my brothers flew out in a rush, leaving feathers scattered thick on the rug.

In the morning my brothers came home. They were muddy, tired, trampled. I gave them cups of coffee and pancakes, eggs, and more coffee. I unlaced their boots, brought them soap and water, helped them into clean clothes. Then, weary-eyed and exhausted, they went off to work.

I cleaned the kitchen, washed the floor. I scrubbed their muddy clothes and put the soup on to simmer until dinner. Then I went to the oak chair in the living room.

My pile of books was waiting. I had discovered them in the attic one night when I couldn't sleep. Old volumes with stiff spines and thick, faded pages that told of men turning into snakes, bears changing into men, birds that flew over prison walls and became young girls, and girls who became birds, who soared in the sky. . . .

The lightness, the flight, the swiftness. The wings, the bills, the small eyes, the haunting cries. The wind and the water. The new dangers. How many times I imagined it all, sitting in my rocking chair. I read and read, often not stopping to eat, until the light dimmed and I heard my brothers' steps on the porch.

Tending daily to my brothers, watching them come in as men and go out as swans, like wheels that turn ceaselessly, I wonder: What is it like to be broken and remade over and over again? And at the moment when they are neither man nor swan, who or what are they?

It seems to me that they are only a breath, only a thought, so fine they could pass through the eye of a needle.

Can I, too, become so fine and smooth, like a piece of silk or a breath of air, that I can turn myself inside out?

One night as they flew out the windows and doors, I felt the breeze from their wings on my face. I heard their cries growing fainter and fainter. And I pictured myself going with them.

I arched my long, narrow throat forward; I stretched my arms wide and I soared over lakes and forests until I found my brothers. When I was tired, I alighted on a rock and my brothers made a circle around me. Then, when we were rested, we rose into the air.

We were like a white necklace flung into the sky. We were like an arrow shot from a bow. We were bound into swans' bodies, but we were free.

I have put away my books, potions, and spells. I am through with frantic searches and impatient questions.

When my brothers change into swans each night, I don't chase after them. I sit quietly in a chair. I close my eyes. I watch the flow of my breath as it travels down my spine and through my arms and legs.

Every night I picture myself with my brothers. Each time I make the journey, I feel closer to them.

It has begun to happen. Already I have felt myself dwindle down to nothing, to darkness, to silence. Once a wing erupted from my arm and a wild cry came out of my throat. Once my body became so light it lifted from the chair. Something is stirring, awakening. A great wing is beating through my days.

THE CHANGELINGS

by Jessica Amanda Salmonson

$\mathbb{A}$ strange creature called the Huluk used to live in Lake Tualatin, now called Wapato Lake, a quiet, shallow lake in Oregon surrounded by gorgeous greenery. The Huluk is not there now, because it outgrew the lake and went to live elsewhere. Today no one sees it; long ago, it was often seen. This story happened in bygone days, when the Huluk still dwelt in that lake.

By nature sluggish, the Huluk waddled like a porcupine when it was out of the water. Its big, flat tail was akin to that of a beaver, but spiked about the rump with enormous quills. It had a long, slender, blunt-ended horn on the top of its round head. The strange horn was flanked by huge clamshell ears. The eyes were two protuberant half-globes, black and moist and never blinking.

The Huluk's horn was covered with red and white spots. The fur of the Huluk was slick and mottled.

Three children were out digging roots one day, a little girl, a little boy, and an older boy. The girl wore a sleeveless dress of seal fur interlaced with braids of mountain-goat wool. Upon her head she wore a bobcat-fur cap. The two boys wore striped coats of tanned deerskin decorated with red beads. When the creature came out of the water, the little boy saw it first. He thought it was a beaver the size of a grizzly bear. He was a fearless boy, and the very idea of such a big beaver made him laugh.

"What are you laughing at?" asked his sister. "What do you see?"

The little boy pointed and exclaimed, "I like that creature's horn! I want it to belong to me!"

When his little sister saw it, she joined in the laughter. The horn was indeed very appealing. Together they ran toward the creature.

"Come back!" cried their older brother, understanding better the dangers of inexplicable beasts. He tried to run after his siblings, but his feet would not move, as though they were stuck in mud, or roots had grabbed him. The little ones did not listen to him.

The Huluk scooped up the little boy on its horn. Then it scooped up the little girl. They were taken into the water. From where the older child was standing, knee-deep in muck, it looked as though his siblings might have been impaled, but he wasn't sure, for they were obviously alive; he could still hear them laughing. As the creature slid into the lake and under the water's surface, carrying the two children on its horn, the older boy's legs were mysteriously freed from the muck, and he turned to flee.

He made it home and told his mother and father, "Brother and Sister have been carried away! The Tualatin lake-monster either drowned them or impaled them, I don't know which!"

Then the boy grew ill. He lay down on a mat in the longhouse. He sweated and moaned. His mother laid over him a cougarskin blanket and, as she did so, she saw that he was covered with red and purple spots.

The children's father was called Wawinxpa. Wawinxpa took a carved box from under a bench in the longhouse and opened it. He drew forth all his best clothes. He dressed himself in a shirt of tanned elkskin that his wife had decorated with beads and quills, tanned leggings and breechcloth, and new moccasins of deerhide with the fur intact.

His marmot-fur knife-belt was decorated with feathers from a white swan's back. His necklace consisted of bear claws, symbolic of warrior strength, plus the rare small shells of a shaman. He blacked his cheeks with pitch soot. Last of all, he put on a headdress. It was made of white swan feathers interspersed with red-and-black woodpecker feathers. The circlet of feathers stuck straight up from his head.

Wawinxpa went to the place where his youngest children had been taken away below the water. At the lake's edge he saw a big hole and followed the Huluk's tracks into a cave. When he came out the other side of the tunnel, he found himself in an enormous dry hollow beneath the lake. As he gazed about, he realized he had entered another world. The sky was made of shimmering earth, and trees were growing downward from the roof of the sky.

Off in the misty distance, he caught a glimpse of his children. They were clinging to the speckled horn of the monster, which trod slowly but steadily away. It moved awkwardly across pitted earth, dragging its tail and gouging the ground with its arrow-length quills, leaving a wide track that was easy to follow.

The father pursued the Huluk and his children through the dismal world, up and down deep gullies. Time and again he caught sight of his children, but the monster was never closer or farther. It was always the same distance away. On the upper bank of the first gulley, Wawinxpa motioned with his hands and cried out for his children to let go of the horn and come to him.

His children clung fast and called back, "Father, we are different, different, different!"

The next day, from the top of the second gulley, he called to them again. But they only replied, "We are different, different!" as they held fast to the Huluk's horn. The monster waddled on and on, and though it never exerted itself, it managed somehow always to keep the same distance. The father grew increasingly despondent.

He made a camp each night in sheltered places low in one or another gulley. Five days he stayed in the strange land. Five times he ascended to a different gulley's ridge and called out, "Come to me, my children, come!" He could never catch up to them, and their reply was always the same.

After the fifth try, the father saw his children no more. He looked everywhere, but the Huluk was nowhere to be seen. Its wide trail vanished on a lava bed. Wawinxpa came out of the cave, into the good world, but the world seemed less good without his children. He went home and told his wife, "The Tualatin monster has taken our children to live under the mountain. All the trees in that place grow straight down out of the sky. I saw our children on the horn of the monster, but could not catch them."

Then he sat down with his wife and together they cried.

The older son lay sick with fever, sleeping fitfully. His mother prepared strong medicinal teas of herbs, crab-apple bark and spruce sap, but nothing helped.

Through the night, Wawinxpa lay near his son. For a long time he could not sleep, for worrying that his last child would die.

Finally, Wawinxpa slept, and his night was filled with dreams. He drew dream-power into himself as he was sleeping. The next day his wife could not wake him. She watched her husband fretfully as she attended her sick son. Toward noon, Wawinxpa opened his eyes and said, "I have seen them in my dream. I will try again to bring them home."

Once more he made himself ready, wearing his many fine garments. He covered his forehead with black pitch. He made speckles on the rest of his face with red paint, white clay, and coal. Then, in the forest, he twisted a long hazel rope and tied one end around his waist. The other end he tied to a tree beside Lake Tualatin. He swam out to the middle of the lake and peered down.

Deep in the clear, clear water he saw his children on the horn of the monster. He called down into the water, "Let go of the horn, my children, and swim up here to me!"

But they replied, "Father, we are different, different, different!"

He swam about the middle of the lake until he was weary, with just the feathers of his headdress sticking up. The whole time he prayed and prayed for assistance from good spirits. He prayed to the clouds, to the lake, to the mountains, to the trees, to the birds, and to the kindly spirit he had met in the forest when he came of age and which was always with him. By then he was so tired that he couldn't even swim to shore. He sank from view. He would have drowned, except that his wife came, dressed in a cedar-bark dress and a robe of inter-woven seal, coon, and bobcat furs. She pulled on the hazel rope, drawing her husband out of the water. She raised him in her arms, wrapped him in a cougar-hide blanket, and held him fast until he was warm.

The next morning, Wawinxpa swam far out into the lake again, with just his headdress of swan and wood-pecker feathers visible from the shore. He called to his children, but their answer was the same as before. On the fifth day, he saw that his children had changed markedly. Their hair was gone. Their eyes were half-globes of darkness without lids. Their bodies had merged into one speckled body with two heads.

He called down to them, "Children, swim up here to me!"

Both heads spoke at once, saying, "Father, I am different, different, different!"

Wawinxpa's five days of prayers, and his rigorous ascetic performance in the lake, assisted in the recovery of his one remaining child. The boy had only white scars to show that the Huluk had seen him. On that last day of the father's prayer, fast, and swimming, the son came with his mother to the lakeshore. Together they pulled on the hazel cord.

For the last time Wawinxpa was drawn out of the water. He clung to his wife and son, and his feather headdress fell to the ground. All he could say was, "The children belong forever to the Huluk. Weep, my wife; weep, my son; weep, for they are different, different, different."

THE TALKING SWORD

by Jack Dann

My name is THE-EDGE-OF-FIRE-AND-DESTINY-THAT-BURNS-AND-CUTS-THROUGH-FLESH, and I'm the demon who's going to set the record straight.

Okay, you can call me FRED-WHO-BURNS-AND-CUTS-THROUGH-FLESH, or if that's too complicated for your little twentieth century brain, you can call me Fred. (I took FIRE and DESTINY and figured that Fred was about as close to my NAME as I could get!) Fred just doesn't quite have the same tone and authority as THE-EDGE-OF-FIRE-AND-DESTINY-THAT-BURNS-AND-CUTS-THROUGH-FLESH, but I'm not a pompous fool like your average demon.

That's because I'm not your average demon.

And don't give me that stupid argument that I'm just a sword! Let me ask you—how many swords have *you* spoken to today?

That's what I thought.

And if you're going to ask me how I got this way, that's for me to know and you to find out. Demons don't have to make excuses. They can take any shape they want. I could be a Hawaiian hula dancer if I want, or a chimpanzee, or a page in this book you're reading.

But why am I bothering to tell you all this?

I could dissolve you in a second! I could cut you to

shreds! I could terrify you! Do you know what my real aspect is? Do you know what I *really* look like?

All right, I'm going to be truthful. I really look like . . . a sword.

My father was a sword, too—a big two-handed *cliadheammor*, which means really big sword in the true tongue. But that's a long story that can wait for another day.

Right now, I'm going to tell you about killing dragons and being a hero. I'm going to tell you exactly how it's done. From A to Z. And—this is the most important—I'm going to show you that the sword is more important than the hero every single time! That's the lesson, so listen up.

But, as you probably know already, there's not a whole lot of room for talking swords and dragons and heroes here in the twentieth century. You got cheated, this is dullsville. You think just because you've got computers that it's all cool. Well, it ain't, as they say. It just simply ain't.

Okay, so now that I've got your attention, it's time to travel.

First we've got to get a hero. We'll find one right here in Melbourne, Australia, a little jerk just like you—all heroes are the same—and then we'll go someplace where there's magic and dragons and no computers! Your choice. I suggest Atlantis around 3600 B.C. or the Göreme region of Turkey around 1466 A.D. Good times and places for magic, although forget about finding dragons on Atlantis. They were wiped out in 2170 B.C. Nah, not by heroes. By a virus. If you're hot to go to the future, best time is anywhere in the thirty-fifth century, anywhere except Southern California—it's too crazy there even for me! And, yeah, they kept their computers.

Okay, one last answer to one last question: there has *always* been time travel. You just have to know where to look. It's been there all the time. I'll give you a hint: go to the library and look up "mnemonics." That's the first clue. If you're smart, you'll find out about the memory theater of Giulio Camillo and Giordano Bruno's secrets of shadows and seals. That's all I'm going to say on the subject. But this time, for this story, the trip is on me. You don't have to know how to do anything.

You've got a sword for a tour guide!

I'm going to take you to a video arcade I know in Melbourne.

Okay, so we're walking down Toorak Road, past all the up-market dress shops and cafés and restaurants, past all the yuppies showing off to all the other yuppies, past all the four-wheel-drive vehicles and Porsches and Mercs and Jags stuck in the rush hour traffic. And just to prove my point about how people don't pay attention to *anything* in this silly century, I'm not changing my aspect, as we call it. None of this invisibility crap for me. And I hate taking the form of clouds or dust or lightning and thunder, or cockatoos or anything else foreign to my primary aspect. See, you're getting the hang of it. If you can speak the language, you can do the tricks.

Can you believe that *nobody* notices that a five-foot-long sword is floating three feet from the pavement and cutting its way down the street? I ask you, how could *anyone* miss a floating sword that's aglow with the unearthly light of Hell and bejeweled with diamonds and rubies and the eyeballs of dead emperors?

You don't know?

Well, *I* do! It's because nobody's paying attention. These yuppies are only worried about being cool and talking into their cellular phones. They're programmed only to see what they're used to seeing.

Yeah, okay so there are a *few* pedestrians who look up and notice that they've just passed a demon shaped like a sword that could cut them into a thousand twitchy, twisty, fleshy, white noodles. But they're too preoccupied with their cool thoughts to remember what they saw. You know, if this place ever got invaded by bug-eyed aliens, nobody would know that anything had happened until the cellular phones stopped working.

If Aragorn's *Narsil-the-Sword-that-Was-Broken* or King Arthur's *Excaliber*, or even Bilbo the Hobbit's *Sting* were here, they'd cut these pedestrians into string! Maybe I should cut a few people up just to show you.

Oh, that would make you sick?

Well, you'll see enough cutting up when our doomed hero fights the dragon.

You ever see dragon's blood? It'll burn the hair right out of your little nose.

* * *

You know what I hate about video arcades? It's the noise. They don't make this much noise in Hell, except in the City of Pluto, and that's mostly filled with people from New York City. (No, dummy, not Pluto the dog; Pluto the prince of darkness, the prince of the under-world, the—oh, forget it.)

So we go right into this video arcade on Toorak Road. It's noisy and big; and for the ultranerds, there's a roller skating rink on the second floor. But our quarry is going to be somewhere in those rows of video machines right in front of us on the first floor. No, not those pin-ball machines that have been souped up to look like video machines. You won't find any heroes playing those, not on your life. No, the heroes want virtual real-ity. They want everything to look as real as technology can make it . . . which ain't very real. Look around at this. This is video city. Video world.

See that nerd with the greasy hair? The one with the pimples and the big stomach that's sticking right out of his baggy jeans? Well, my fellow traveler, all the heroes start out like that. Really. They all need baths and sham-poos and diets. You think I'm making this up? You should have seen Hercules before we fixed him up. Looked just like this nerd, except he wore a dress in-stead of jeans. Well, everybody wore dresses then.

See the game he's playing?

It's called *Dragons' Teeth*. See, our potential hero is pretending that he's the muscle guy with the sword that's as big as my father. He's whacking everyone with the sword. Now that he's whacked everyone, killed everyone in sight, everything that moves, he's won the right to play another screen. Now he gets to kill dragons. *Swish, slash*, look at him, he's really into it. He's breathing heavily, his eyes are glazed. He thinks all this virtual killing is cool. He'd kill his grandmother if she appeared on the screen.

Well, let's see how he feels about the real thing.

"Hey, you. Yah, you, the fat kid playing *Dragons' Teeth*. Too involved in the game to listen?"

How about that? He doesn't seem to hear me, so there's nothing to do, but put myself into his hands, so to speak. So I float right into his pudgy little paws. There, little nerd—now you're holding THE-EDGE-OF-FIRE-AND-DESTINY-THAT-BURNS-AND-CUTS-THROUGH-FLESH, and this is the part I love the best. *Smash!* I cut into the machine, and sparks fly all over and lights go out all over the arcade and whatever I strike catches fire, and lightning shoots from my blade, careening all over the place like superballs, and flames crackle and smoke billows and everyone is screaming, and the nerd can't let go of me, and he's trying to scream, too, but I'm not going to let anything come out of his mouth. He's my slave. He's under my power.

Like you. So stop the screaming. You're under my *protection*.

Now, little nerd, start swinging. We'll smash all the machines in the place. See how quiet it is now that everyone has run out the doors. I don't even hear the skating Muzak coming from upstairs. Of course the ceiling's on fire. Oh, don't worry about the police. All they'll see is a circle of blue fire, which will scare the snot out of them.

One by one we smash every machine in the place. Pluto would have been proud, although I doubt Walt Disney would have approved.

"Okay, kid," I say to our potential hero, "that's enough. You can relax now. You don't have to stand there shaking with your arms sticking out. I'm over here, in front of you. Hanging magically in the air. I'm the sword. Hello...hello? There, now. That's better. Tell us your name."

"Haaa—Harrrrahrrr . . ."

"Is that all you can say? Come on, spit it out!"

"Hhhhharold Waaag—"

"Come on, Hhhhharold, you can do it."

"Harold Wagner," he says. Clear as a bell.

"There, I told you, you could do it. Harold. Hmm. Harold the Hero. Hey, that sounds pretty good. Now, Harold the Hero, stop shaking. And stop that coughing. Don't you *want* to be a hero?"

He shakes his head, of course. They all do that when they're called to greatness. Shaking like a leaf—it's the stuff of heroes.

"Would you like to run away?"

Now he nods.

"Okay," I say. "Go on, then, get your bum out of here. Bye, bye. It's been nice smashing things up with you. But wouldn't you rather stay with us and be a hero?"

See how he strains to run down the aisle and get

away from us demons. Well, if he had any muscles, they'd be straining. Yeah, he thinks *you're* a demon, too. This is the way it works, kid—he gets to be a hero and you get to be a demon. Fun, huh?

"Okay, Harold, stop shaking and sweating. You can't move. You're in my power. And you're going to be in my power until you're a great, big, strapping hero. What do you think of that? That's right, you can just nod."

See, he's nodding.

Now all I have to do is put myself back in his hands ever so and lead him to his training grounds. "Hey, Harold, want to kill some dragons?"

He nods, tears flowing down his cheeks.

"Good."

Now, what's it to be: Göreme in 1466 A.D., Atlantis in 3600 B.C., or any place in the thirty-fifth century except Southern California?

Göreme it is, then.

Just close your eyes.

Time travel ain't nothing but a state of mind.

So you think all this hero stuff is cruel and inhuman?

Well, I'm a demon. What did you expect, *Fantasia*?

Okay, okay, you can open your eyes now. We've arrived. This is it. Well, this is almost it. Tell me what you see in front of you. (I don't care if it makes you hungry and thirsty, just tell me what you see. And don't give me any lip about how I'm torturing Harold the Hero. That's what I'm *supposed* to be doing.)

Since the cat's got your tongue, I'll tell you what to see. Okay, behind you—that's right, turn around—behind you are the sacred cones and stones and mounds and churches and desert of Göreme. Surprise, it's all desert—no water, no rain, no liquid of any kind, unless you know where to look. Of course, you can always just find a dragon, slay the thing, and then drink its ichor. It's purple and spicy and tastes like puke, but it's good for you.

You don't know what ichor is?

It's dragon's blood, dummy!

Of course, this place looks weird. Do you think dragons would live in suburban Sydney, or even in the outback? Nah. Weird monsters need very weird places. Just plain weird won't quite do it. See all the strange rocks that look like cones, that seem to go on forever? They're called *peri bacalari*. That means "fairy chimneys." You're looking right into the sacred region of Ürgüp, and the local people believe that a thousand spirits dwell in there. They're wrong, though. Last time I counted, eight thousand, three hundred and forty-seven spirits were living in those cone fields. You'd better watch yourself, though, because according to the legends, the spirits fall in love with children and steal them away.

I'm not going to tell you whether the legends are true. That's for me to know and you to find out!

But if you look carefully, you can see the spirits drifting around. See, they look like smoke, and if you keep looking you can see their shapes. Don't stare at them like you're trying to thread a needle or you won't see anything! Can you see them now? Pretty ugly and horrible, huh? I always thought they looked like part spider and part octopus. Well, if you think the spirits are ugly, you should see the monsters that live *inside* the cones! The monsters are flesh and blood just like the dragons. They'd eat your eyes right out of your head and save the rest of you for lunch. You don't have to worry so much about the monsters while you're with me, but one of those spirits might just drift over here and grab you!

After all, you're awfully cute.

Okay, *now* you can turn around. That's right, turn around and look at Harold the Hero. I suppose you're wondering how Harold the Hero ended up right in the middle of that beautiful pool of water, huh? And I suppose you're wondering how that beautiful pool of water ended up in the middle of the desert? It's an oasis, dummy. Didn't you ever see any movies like *Lawrence of Arabia*? Yeah, it's pretty obvious that Harold isn't happy in there, especially with all those scrumptious trees hanging over him with pears, figs, apples, and pomegranates.

I love this part. See how every time he tries to grab one of those pieces of fruit, the wind blows them out of his reach? This is all part of Harold's training. I got the idea from an old Greek god named Zeus who got upset with his son Tantalus and stuck him into this very pool. I figured it's a great way to turn nerds into heroes. Can you think of a better way to lose weight and get exercise?

See, there he goes again, reaching for a fig. He'll be skinny as a rail before he manages to grab one of those fruits. Watch this. . . .

"Hey, Harold the Hero. Aren't you thirsty?" I have to shout at him because when you're in the pool, you can't see beyond the fruit trees, and you can't hear so well in there, either.

There, Harold's looking this way.

"Try to drink the water, Harold. You'll get dehydrated from all that exercise. Go ahead, try it."

Harold is bending over, trying to get a drink of that water, but the farther he bends, the lower the pool sinks. I love that! "Hey, Harold, try again."

Harold snarls at me like an angry dog. See that? Now you and I know that swords don't have bums, but it's good that he's getting angry. And if he keeps reaching for those fruits and bending over for a drink, he'll get some exercise, too. And every once in a while, the wind won't blow and he'll get a fig or a pomegranate. And every once in a while he'll bend over and the water won't sink.

You see, I'm not such a bad sort after all.

Okay, we don't have lots of time, so we're going to speed things up. Time is elastic. You can pull it like taffy or squash it like your twentieth century bread. (Oh, you haven't tried that? If you take a loaf of supermarket white bread and squeeze it, you'll end up with nothing more than a little ball of sticky stuff. That's because the garbage you call bread is mostly air.) Anyway, let's speed things up for Harold the Hero.

Okay, *zap*, *boom*, *whiz*, a few months have passed.
Now look at Harold.

He's thin and wiry and you can see the muscles in his arms and the definition in his pecs. He's becoming a regular Hercules, isn't he? He's even got a cleft in his chin like all proper heroes. He can see us now. Well, he can see me, anyway. Listen.

"Hey, Harold, how you doin' in there?"

"Get me out of here, you—"

"That ain't nice, Harold. You should always treat a sword with respect. And here I was going to get you out of there so you could slay a dragon and become a real hero. Oh, well. I guess I'll come back in a few months."

"No, don't go, I'm sorry, I—"

Zap. We'll push time forward real quick. You see, before you can say "Jack Robinson," a month has passed.

"Hey, Harold, how you doin' in there?"

"Fine," says Harold, very politely this time.

"You ready to get out and learn to fight dragons?"

"Yeah, I guess."

"You guess?" I say. "That's not the way a hero talks to his sword."

"Yes, yes, I'm ready to learn. I'm ready to do anything. Just please get me out of here."

"Are you going to have respect for your sword?"

"Yes."

"Are you going to do everything I tell you?"

"Yes."

"Promise?"

"I promise."

"And do you know what will happen if you misbehave?"

Harold really is turning into a hero. See how his face has lost all that baby fat? See how all his ugly red, pustulating pimples have disappeared? (That's what happens when you stop eating candy bars and all the fast food crap.) He's actually quite handsome now, isn't he?

"Yes," Harold says, answering my question about whether he knows what will happen if he misbehaves.

"You do?" I ask.

"Yessir."

"Then tell me what you think will happen."

"I'll have to stand here in the pool until I learn how to behave."

"No, Harold. If you misbehave, I'm going to let the dragons roast you for barbecue and eat your fatty entrails. And then I'll go and find another hero who *will* behave. Do I make myself clear?"

"Yessir," Harold says.

That's my boy!

Okay, listen up. Harold's been doing dragon training now for another two months, even though that's barely a nanosecond to us. Harold knows almost everything there is to know about killing dragons and being a hero. After all, he's got a good teacher. But is he happy? Ask him.

"Harold, are you happy?"

Harold looks right at me. He's a regular Hercules. Look at those muscles. You'd never in a million years guess that when we found him, he was a nerd playing video games in an arcade. But he doesn't say anything. He's scared. He doesn't look it, but he's still the same nerd we found in that video game arcade. Come closer: I'm going to tell you a secret. All those movie stars and athletes that you think are so cool—they're nerds, too.

They just don't act like nerds. That's their secret.

"C'mon, Harold, old hero, answer the question. Are you happy?"

Harold nods his head.

Of course, he's happy. If he wasn't happy, I'd throw him back in the pool again or just feed him to the dragons.

Okay, it's time to maim and kill.

Let's find our hero some dragons.

Before we journey through the fairy cones and past the hungry spirits who just *love* children, you need to know something about dragons. Harold knows what he's got to do, but you need to know something too, because a dragon could just as easily decide to take a bite of you as fight Harold. So be warned.

Okay, a dragon is just another name for a worm. That's right, it's just a great big worm. (Actually, dragons got their name from the old Greek word *draca*, which means "serpent" or "worm".) And just in case you're stupid enough to think that dragons aren't real, think about this: How do you think that Drakelow in England got its name? It means "dragon's barrow." And have you ever heard of the towns of Drakeford or Dragon's Hill in England? Or Drakensberg, which means "dragon's mountain," in Germany? Or Draconis in southeastern Europe? You can look those places up in the atlas. All those towns were named after dragons because they were plagued with them. So don't let anyone give you a hard time about how dragons are legends.

There are all kinds of dragons, but the ones that live here in Turkey are the wingless and legless worms called *D. cappadociae*. They have only one head, unlike *D. ladonii*, which have a hundred. But don't think that killing them is a piece of cake just because they have only one head and can't fly. They can crawl faster than you can run, they breathe fire, salivate green stringy bile that melts flesh, are covered with scales that a guided missile couldn't penetrate, have forty-four diamond shark's teeth, and they smell like a fart.

You'll smell the dragon before you see it.

Okay, onward through the fields of Göreme, past the thousands of fairy chimneys that look like tents made out of rocks; onward, past the houses and churches carved right out of the stratified rocks by the early Christian fathers, past Turkish villages turned black by dragon flames and dragon farts. (Ah, you didn't know about dragon farts; well, *that's* a story for another day, kid.)

Yuk! Can you smell that? Makes old Harold smell like perfume, doesn't it? (Well, Harold's wearing full dress armor, and that stuff ain't cotton. You try wearing body armor and see if you don't smell like essence of fart, too!)

There's definitely a dragon out there, beyond the vast plain of rock towers ahead of us. See the smoke? You wait; in a while the whole sky will turn black and red, and the clouds will look like they're made out of soot. All we've got to do is keep walking. The dragon knows we're here. How? It's a worm, like I told you. It *feels* us through the ground like a bunch of little vibrations. And you aren't exactly tiptoeing. Dragons have pretty good eyes, too. By now it can probably even see us, although we can't see it.

"Harold, are you ready?" I ask. "You know what you have to do?"

Harold nods. He's leading the way, all dressed up in armor, sweating like a pig, carrying a heavy dragon shield that he wouldn't have even been able to pick up a few months ago, and he's actually acting like a hero.

Of course, he hasn't seen the dragon yet.

Let me tell you a few more things. I've taught Harold about how to hold a sword, how to parry, riposte, lunge, cut, thrust, feint, so he knows some technique, which he'll need if I happen to be on vacation and he has to fight a dragon by himself. You see, being a hero when you've got a sword (not just a sword sword, but a demon sword like me) is a piece of cake. The sword does all the work. It pulls you around (providing you're not so fat that you can't move!), it knows how to lead the dragon on, it knows how to confuse the stupid beast with techniques learned over millennia, and most important, it knows how to kill the dragon. Ah, you think that's an easy thing?

Wait till you see the dragon. . . .

And there it is.

It slithers right for us at maybe a hundred miles an hour, burrowing through the sand, sending it flying all over; and its breath is so hot that it turns the sand into glass all around it, leaving a trail of glass that reflects the sun like a mirror. It stops right in front of Harold and pulls itself up like a python to full height. Its scales look like precious stones, like blood-red rubies; but its head, which looks like the head of a huge fly, is covered with something that looks like layers and layers of puke and snot. If that stuff drips on you, you'll melt, I guarantee it. And its huge green eyes stare down at us as steadily as a crocodile watching its prey. It takes a deep breath and is about to turn everybody into barbecue.

"Harold, lift up your shield, dummy!"

Harold raises the shield as fire pours down upon us, but that shield is pretty powerful stuff, and the dragon-flame breaks against the shield and turns into smoke and soot, so you probably can hardly see what's going on now. I leap into Harold's hand, and now you'll see what heroes are made of. Real heroes are the dummies. They hold the sword. It's the sword who does the fighting! But first I've got to get behind this stupid dragon, and maybe the dragon isn't so stupid because it's keeping its snotty, vomit-gooped head right in front of me.

"Now, Harold, remember what I taught you. Feint to the left, roll, keep that shield up or I'll be fighting the dragon alone—and watch it, it's dripping bile, you want to get us both melted?"

Okay, I should ask you something, even though we're right in the middle of fighting the dragon . . . even though all this green dragon bile is falling all around us. (If enough of that stuff touches Harold—or me!—it could dissolve us as easily as aspirin melts in water.) So, listen up. Here's an easy question: If I'm doing all the fighting, why do I need a hero?

Because it's *traditional*, dummy!

And it gives you humans something to do!

Now that that's settled, back to the fight.

Oops, I warned you that dragons are dangerous. It feinted, swung its wormy neck around Harold and me, and turned everything to glass behind us.

"Okay, Harold, now's your chance. Run to the left quickly. I only need a second. There it is. See the spot right in the middle of the dragon's back? See the gray, wormy flesh where there're no scales? JUMP!

"I got it, I'm burying myself right into its flesh. Yuk, I hate this part! Well, you can help pull me out of this blasted dragon. PULL! Okay, now back off because it's going to catch fire and—"

The thing explodes.

Fire shoots everywhere.

Dragon scales rip through the air like shrapnel.

Dragon flesh drops into the sand like puke-covered boulders.

And it doesn't smell too pleasant, either.

"Congratulations, Harold. One dragon bites the dust . . . er, the sand! Harold? Harold?"

Well, kid, this was his first time. He's allowed to shake and snivel and cry.

The dragon is dead, so you can stop all that shaking and sniveling and crying, too. So, your arm got burnt by a little bit of dragon bile. Big deal! Don't complain, you didn't even dissolve.

What a crybaby!

This is known in literary talk as the denouement. That means it's the final outcome. This is where I wrap everything up so you can go home. Or what's left of you, anyway.

Harold will keep shaking in his armor every time we fight a dragon for the next few years. But he'll figure things out, and we'll probably work out pretty well as a team. Then he'll get a big head and think he's a big shot or, worse, he'll fall in love with a damsel in distress, that sort of thing. He'll actually believe he knows enough to kill dragons without my help. After all, he'll be able to travel around wherever he wants in time. You could, too, if you'd go to the library and figure it all out like I suggested.

So what will *I* do?

Well, I'll probably work on my own for a while, then get myself a new hero.

But, you know what I've been thinking about a lot lately?

I might just take a break and go into computer pro-
gramming. I could design some mean video games.
How about something like a game called *The Talking
Sword*?

Why not?

After all, even demons need to make a few dollars
now and then.

I've had my eye on one of those cellular phones for a
while. And I might even buy a new Jag.

Of course, I'd have to grow some arms and hands.
But that's no problem.

I'm a demon, after all. . . .

FREEDOM

by Connie Wilkins

I'm not the only one who sees the wolves. Sometimes the prey sees them, the last thing it ever sees, but I'm not just talking about rats and fat slow pigeons and winos. A few others can look at them and not through them, and I used to wonder what we had in common, and whether it was a power or a weakness.

Anybody can see their stone shells, of course, if they look high enough above West 30th Street near Seventh Avenue. I live on the nineteenth floor, and for six months after the crash nothing seemed more worth doing than staring across the city canyon at the rows and rows of carved wolf heads.

I never found out, even when I could finally maneuver my wheels around the public library, whose idea it had been to decorate the top ten floors of The Fur Exchange building with lifelike heads of wolves. Were they supposed to *protect* the place where their pelts were sold? Or curse it? Whichever, most of the fur traders are long gone now.

But the wolves are still there, beautiful and wild. If they were ever trapped they have found their way free. And I thought that since I could see them, watch them drift in misty swirls down to the distant pavement and form into sinuous night-hunters, I should be able to find my own way free.

If there *was* any freedom for me. In my darkest moments, I dreamed of transforming into a four-legged hunter—only to find that two of those legs were still too crippled to let me walk.

Then Rizpah came and blew my black moods away for good. From the moment she lurched into the elevator bent under a backpack half her own size, I knew she looked *at* me, not through me. When I finally decided to meet her eyes, she flushed a little, but there was determination behind her shyness.

"Hi . . . I'm Rizpah. You're Lucas, aren't you? I asked Alonzo-the-doorman. I hope you don't mind."

I did mind that she must have seen me being hoisted up the lift into the school van, but there was no point in holding that against her.

"No problem. You just move in here?"

"Yeah, twelfth floor. You're on nineteen?"

She *had* been doing research, hadn't she! I didn't have time to decide whether I minded or not before she blurted out, fast and nervous, "You must have a better view of . . . of the wolves from there."

"Pretty good," I said casually. "Come up some time and have a look." Then, as the elevator stopped on the first floor, I added, "Hang that megapack on the back of my chair and I'll give it a ride as far as the curb."

"Thanks!" She didn't object, didn't hesitate, just slung the straps over the chair handles and let me show off. I zipped across the lobby, using the weight of her pack to tilt backward as I took the three wide stairs down to street level. Alonzo flashed me a grin and got the door open just in time.

"Hey, remind me never to arm-wrestle with you!" Rizpah said when she caught up. "Okay if I come up this afternoon? To see the wolves?"

"Sure, I'll be home by three." And then I watched her stride away, her long, tawny ponytail swishing over that absurd backpack. I flexed my gloved hands, gripped the wheels again, and rolled toward the van pulling up at the curb. I was just as glad she wasn't watching now, but I already knew it didn't matter.

By late afternoon, we were leaning together on my windowsill as daylight shaded to dusk. We'd talked about schools, movies, regular-world stuff, but now there was no need to talk. I could tell by her stillness, by the intensity in her greenish eyes, that she could see what I saw.

When the swirls of mist began to drift downward and take shape far below, I handed her my binoculars. After a minute or two she murmured, almost to herself, "If you can see them through these, they must be real, right? How could lenses bend and magnify illusions? But the people walking down there don't seem to see a thing."

"Once in a while somebody does," I answered. "Usually somebody already a little crazy, but not always. Alonzo-the-doorman can see them, and he seemed to know without asking that I could, too."

She handed the binoculars back; the glint in her narrowed eyes gave her a feline look. "Have you ever gone down there, among them?"

"Just waiting for the right time. I guess this is it."

She met my challenge without hesitation. Ten minutes later, we were crossing 30th Street.

Either one of us alone might have felt afraid. Rizpah's hand, clenched on the armrest of my chair, was white around the knuckles, and an icy tingle shivered across my skin, more excitement than fear.

A few mist-swirls still drifted downward as we approached. Their solidifying shapes curved into a smoky semicircle as though to dare us, or maybe invite us, to enter. Then we were among them, and the gap closed, and the outer world became faded and insubstantial. Our reality was the ripple of silver-gray fur, and the sidelong glance of yellow eyes as the wolves circled us.

One wolf, bigger than the others, stepped inside the circle and stared directly at us. We stared back. I felt Rizpah's side pressed against my chair, her body absolutely still while her muscles tensed for action, but I felt strangely calm now. When the alpha wolf sniffed at my hand I pulled off my glove and stretched the hand out. He closed his jaws gently around it, and then pressed down, not so gently, as I willed myself to relax in his grip.

Rizpah stiffened even more. I glanced up at her in warning, and saw her green eyes glowing like the wolves' eyes. I wondered what my eyes looked like right now.

Just as I felt a trickle of blood between my knuckles the wolf let my hand go. He swung his head toward Rizpah, sniffed at her hand, showed his gleaming teeth in a wide yawn, or grin, or both—then he turned away and the wolves melted into the dusk, spreading out through city trails on the nightly hunt.

"They accept us!" I said, and only then realized that Rizpah had gripped my arm so hard it hurt.

"Lucas . . . what do they know about us?" she asked in a strained voice. "I've always felt different from most people, and I knew right away that you were different, too, but why? What are we supposed to do now?"

"Just wait, I guess. And watch."

But of course we couldn't just watch. The next evening, and the next, and whenever we could for weeks, we went among the wolves at dusk and tried to follow them on the hunt. Sometimes they seemed to humor us and let us keep up for a while, but even my wheels couldn't match their easy lope when they got going. Anyway, I couldn't leave Rizpah behind and alone on the city streets at night.

Sometimes they brought prey back with them. I wondered whether there were cubs tucked away in niches in the ornate stonework far above. Usually the wolves just faded into the walls at street level, prey and all, when they returned. But one night, the alpha wolf came right up to me and dropped a fat pigeon in my lap. Then, with that sly yawn/laugh, he turned away. His tail was still brushing me as his nose disappeared into solid stone.

"How come you rate?" Rizpah asked when she stopped gaping.

"It helps to have a permanent lap," I said. "And maybe he figures you could always eat that cat food you lug around in your pack for strays. But I'm willing to share."

I was only half joking. A strange hunger gripped me as I felt the weight of the still-warm bird in my lap. My skin tingled, as though something—fur?—wanted to grow from it.

"Maybe we should . . . experiment . . . in private," Rizpah murmured. I knew from her voice that she felt as weird as I did.

We did share. After considerable discussion, we cooked the bird first. Not because the idea of raw meat bothered us, but because of horror stories about diseases in city pigeons. It's a good thing my mother works nights because neither of us had ever plucked and gutted a bird, and the kitchen was pretty gross for a while.

Maybe it was because we cooked the pigeon instead of eating it raw, maybe not, but nothing much happened afterward. I'm not sure what we'd expected. We were blaming and practically snarling at each other by the time Rizpah had to go home. We had seemed so close to something. . . .

When she finally stormed out the door, she hissed nastily, "Don't fool yourself. You'll never be a wolf!" Then, halfway down the hall, she turned. "Something, I think, but not a wolf." Her forehead was puckered as though she didn't know herself what she meant, and the anger was gone from her voice.

*   *   *

101

Next day, I watched the street corner from my window, waiting for Rizpah to appear. She was a lot later than usual, and I wondered whether she was holding a grudge; I'd been at least as nasty as she had.

I don't know how long I'd been looking when I realized that, even without binoculars, everything nineteen stories below was as clear to me as if I were at street level. I pushed the window farther open and pulled myself onto the sill enough to look straight down.

Heights have never scared me. Now the sea of air seemed to call to me, and things below looked clear but dull and insignificant. I glanced upward, and the tall buildings seemed to challenge me to look down on their summits.

My arms quivered, but not because of my weight on them. They were easily strong enough from all my self-propelled wheeling. I wanted . . . but I couldn't form a clear image of what I wanted, or any idea of what to do about it.

A sudden metallic *clang* drew my attention back down. Then came another, and another, as a car swerved drunkenly back and forth along the street, banging fenders on parked cars as it went. Nothing I hadn't seen before, but usually late at night. It was only four-thirty. . . .

I glanced toward the corner, and the jaunty bounce of Rizpah's ponytail caught my eye. She was jogging toward the crossing, trying to make the "walk" light. But the drunk driver was still lurching along the cross street. He wasn't going to stop. . . .

I pushed off into space, and the air grasped me, stripping away everything I had been. I felt searing pain, exhilaration, the rush of wind past and through my being. Air tore at me, filled me, forced chambers in my very bones, and I exploded into truth, and freedom.

No time to think . . . falling wasn't fast enough. Power surged through the wings that had been arms. Three times they thrust with all their strength against the resisting air, then closed against my streamlined body as I dove, ripping a hole through space and time.

Rizpah looked up, still moving forward in that smooth lope of hers, just before I struck. My transformation had shrunk me to the size of a peregrine falcon, no more than a foot and a half, beak to tail, but the force was more than enough to knock her backward to the sidewalk.

She yelled, started to scramble up, then saw the car crumpled against the street sign just where she would have stepped next. She sank back to the pavement.

I saw and heard, but by then her face was a pale, dwindling oval far below. She stared up into the sky, and her cry of "Luca-a-a-s" reached me and twined into my consciousness just enough to imprint on me why I might return.

Then I was soaring and diving, tasting the freedom of the vast sea of air with every atom of my body. Far below me, the earthbound city huddled, dwarfed by the curve of the great harbor and the darkening ocean beyond.

To the west, the land stretched into haze tinged red

and gold by sunset. Still I rode the sky, not tiring, but as dusk spread, the lights of the city beckoned. At last I drifted down toward home and the outstretched arm of the girl who waited at my window.

Changing back was slower and less painful, but we didn't go out among the wolves that night. We watched, though, and the eyes of each stone head seemed to glow and stare briefly into ours just before their spirits descended in swirls of mist.

"Can you do it again, whenever you want? Even when you don't have to . . . to save anybody?" Rizpah was still shaken by it all. Well, so was I, of course, but I had no doubts.

"Oh, yeah! I just lean into the air, let it fill me . . ."

"Do you think I could—"

"No! Don't even think about it! You're not a falcon, you're . . . something different. When the time comes, you'll know."

I knew already, but I wasn't about to tell her. I had glimpsed her true nature before without understanding it, in the way she moved, the way her green eyes narrowed and glinted when she was excited, the way she always carried food for strays. When her time came, I was going to make sure to be well out of range with room to fly. We'd work it out in the long run, but the first encounter between hawk and wildcat might be . . . well . . . interesting.

FEVER DREAM

by Ray Bradbury

They put him between fresh, clean, laundered sheets and there was always a newly squeezed glass of thick orange juice on the table under the dim pink lamp. All Charles had to do was call and Mom or Dad would stick their heads into his room to see how sick he was. The acoustics of the room were fine; you could hear the toilet gargling its porcelain throat of mornings, you could hear the rain tap the roof or sly mice run in the secret walls or the canary singing in its cage downstairs. If you were very alert, sickness wasn't too bad.

He was thirteen, Charles was. It was mid-September, with the land beginning to burn with autumn. He lay in the bed for three days, before the terror overcame him.

His hand began to change. His right hand. He looked at it and it was hot and sweating right there on the counterpane alone. It fluttered, it moved a bit. Then it lay there, changing color.

That afternoon the doctor came again and tapped his thin chest like a little drum. "How are you?" asked the doctor, smiling. "I know, don't tell me: 'My *cold* is fine, Doctor, but *I* feel awful!' Ha!" He laughed at his own oft-repeated joke.

Charles lay there and for him that terrible and ancient jest was becoming a reality. The joke fixed itself in

106

his mind. His mind touched and drew away from it in a pale terror. The doctor did not know how cruel he was with his jokes! "Doctor," whispered Charles, lying flat and colorless. "My *hand*, it doesn't *belong* to me any more. This morning it *changed* into something else. I want you to change it back, Doctor, Doctor!"

The doctor showed his teeth and patted his hand. "It looks fine to me, son. You just had a little fever dream."

"But it changed, Doctor, oh, Doctor," cried Charles, pitifully holding up his pale wild hand. "It *did!*"

The doctor winked. "I'll give you a pink pill for that." He popped a tablet onto Charles' tongue. "Swallow!"

"Will it make my hand change back and become *me*, again?"

"Yes, yes."

The house was silent when the doctor drove off down the road in his car under the quiet, blue September sky. A clock ticked far below in the kitchen world. Charles lay looking at his hand.

It did not change back. It was still something else.

The wind blew outside. Leaves fell against the cool window.

At four o'clock his other hand changed. It seemed almost to become a fever. It pulsed and shifted, cell by cell. It beat like a warm heart. The fingernails turned blue and then red. It took about an hour for it to change and when it was finished, it looked just like any ordinary hand. But it was not ordinary. It no longer was him any more. He lay in a fascinated horror and then fell into an exhausted sleep.

Mother brought the soup up at six. He wouldn't touch it. "I haven't any hands," he said, eyes shut.

"Your hands are perfectly good," said mother.

"No," he wailed. "My hands are gone. I feel like I have stumps. Oh, Mama, Mama, hold me, hold me, I'm scared!"

She had to feed him herself.

"Mama," he said, "get the doctor, please, again. I'm so sick."

"The doctor'll be here tonight at eight," she said, and went out.

At seven, with night dark and close around the house, Charles was sitting up in bed when he felt the thing happening to first one leg and then the other. "Mama! Come quick!" he screamed.

But when mama came the thing was no longer happening.

When she went downstairs, he simply lay without fighting as his legs beat and beat, grew warm, red-hot, and the room filled with the warmth of his feverish change. The glow crept up from his toes to his ankles and then to his knees.

"May I come in?" The doctor smiled in the doorway.

"Doctor!" cried Charles. "Hurry, take off my blankets!"

The doctor lifted the blankets tolerantly. "There you are. Whole and healthy. Sweating, though. A little fever. I told you not to move around, bad boy." He pinched the moist pink cheek. "Did the pills help? Did your hand change back?"

"No, no, now it's my other hand and my legs!"

"Well, well, I'll have to give you three more pills, one for each limb, eh, my little peach?" laughed the doctor.

"Will they help me? Please, please. What've I *got?*"

"A mild case of scarlet fever, complicated by a slight cold."

"Is it a germ that lives and has more little germs in me?"

"Yes."

"Are you *sure* it's scarlet fever? You haven't taken any tests!"

"I guess I know a certain fever when I see one," said the doctor, checking the boy's pulse with cool authority.

Charles lay there, not speaking until the doctor was crisply packing his black kit. Then in the silent room, the boy's voice made a small, weak pattern, his eyes alight with remembrance. "I read a book once. About petrified trees, wood turning to stone. About how trees fell and rotted and minerals got in and built up and they look just like trees, but they're not, they're stone." He stopped. In the quiet warm room his breathing sounded.

"Well?" asked the doctor.

"I've been thinking," said Charles after a time. "Do germs ever get big? I mean, in biology class they told us about one-celled animals, amoebas and things, and how millions of years ago they got together until there was a bunch and they made the first body. And more and more cells got together and got bigger and then finally maybe there was a fish and finally here *we* are, and all we are is a bunch of cells that decided to get together, to help each other out. Isn't that right?" Charles wet his feverish lips.

Ray Bradbury

"What's this all about?" The doctor bent over him.

"I've got to tell you this. Doctor, oh, I've got to!" he cried. "What would happen, oh just pretend, please pretend, that just like in the old days, a lot of microbes got together and wanted to make a bunch, and reproduced and made *more*—"

His white hands were on his chest now, crawling toward his throat.

"And they decided to *take over* a person!" cried Charles.

"Take over a person?"

"Yes, *become* a person. *Me*, my hands, my feet! What if a disease somehow knew how to kill a person and yet live after him?"

He screamed.

His hands were on his neck.

The doctor moved forward, shouting.

At nine o'clock the doctor was escorted out to his car by the mother and father, who handed him his bag. They conversed in the cool night wind for a few minutes. "Just be sure his hands are kept strapped to his legs," said the doctor. "I don't want him hurting himself."

"Will he be all right, Doctor?" The mother held to his arm a moment.

He patted her shoulder. "Haven't I been your family physician for thirty years? It's the fever. He imagines things."

"But those bruises on his throat, he almost choked himself."

110

"Just you keep him strapped; he'll be all right in the morning."

The car moved off down the dark September road.

At three in the morning, Charles was still awake in his small black room. The bed was damp under his head and his back. He was very warm. Now he no longer had any arms or legs, and his body was beginning to change. He did not move on the bed, but looked at the vast blank ceiling space with insane concentration. For a while he had screamed and thrashed, but now he was weak and hoarse from it, and his mother had gotten up a number of times to soothe his brow with a wet towel. Now he was silent, his hands strapped to his legs.

He felt the walls of his body change, the organs shift, the lungs catch fire like burning bellows of pink alcohol. The room was lighted up as with the flickerings of the hearth.

Now he had no body. It was all gone. It was under him, but it was filled with a vast pulse of some burning, lethargic drug. It was as if a guillotine had neatly lopped off his head, and his head lay shining on a midnight pillow while the body, below, still alive, belonged to somebody else. The disease had eaten his body and from the eating had reproduced itself in feverish duplicate. There were the little hand hairs and the fingernails and the scars and the toenails and the tiny mole on his right hip, all done again in perfect fashion.

I am dead, he thought. I've been killed and yet I live. My body is dead, it is all disease and nobody will know.

111

I will walk around and it will not be me, it will be something else. It will be something all bad, all evil, so big and so evil it's hard to understand or think about. Something that will buy shoes and drink water and get married some day maybe and do more evil in the world than has ever been done.

Now the warmth was stealing up his neck, into his cheeks, like a hot wine. His lips burned, his eyelids, like leaves, caught fire. His nostrils breathed out blue flame, faintly, faintly.

This will be all, he thought. It'll take my head and my brain and fix each eye and every tooth and all the marks in my brain, and every hair and every wrinkle in my ears, and there'll be nothing left of me.

He felt his brain fill with a boiling mercury. He felt his left eye clench in upon itself and, like a snail, withdraw, shift. He was blind in his left eye. It no longer belonged to him. It was enemy territory. His tongue was gone, cut out. His left cheek was numbed, lost. His left ear stopped hearing. It belonged to someone else now. This thing that was being born, this mineral thing replacing the wooden log, this disease replacing healthy animal cell.

He tried to scream and he was able to scream loud and high and sharply in the room, just as his brain flooded down, his right eye and ear were cut out, he was blind and deaf, all fire, all terror, all panic, all death.

His scream stopped before his mother ran through the door to his side.

*   *   *

112

It was a good, clear morning, with a brisk wind that helped carry the doctor up the path before the house. In the window above, the boy stood, fully dressed. He did not wave when the doctor waved and called, "What's this? Up? My God!"

The doctor almost ran upstairs. He came gasping into the bedroom.

"What are you doing out of bed?" he demanded of the boy. He tapped his thin chest, took his pulse and temperature. "Absolutely amazing! Normal. Normal, by God!"

"I shall never be sick again in my life," declared the boy, quietly, standing there, looking out the wide window. "Never."

"I hope not. Why, you're looking fine, Charles."

"Doctor?"

"Yes, Charles?"

"Can I got to school *now?*" asked Charles.

"Tomorrow will be time enough. You sound positively eager."

"I am. I like school. All the kids. I want to play with them and wrestle with them, and spit on them and play with the girls' pigtails and shake the teacher's hand, and rub my hands on all the cloaks in the cloakroom, and I want to grow up and travel and shake hands with people all over the world, and be married and have lots of children, and go to libraries and handle books and—*all* of that I want to!" said the boy, looking off into the September morning. "What's the name you called me?"

"What?" The doctor was puzzled. "I called you nothing but Charles."

"It's better than no name at all, I guess." The boy shrugged.

"I'm glad you want to go back to school," said the doctor.

"I really anticipate it," smiled the boy. "Thank you for your help, Doctor. Shake hands."

"Glad to."

They shook hands gravely, and the clear wind blew through the open window. They shook hands for almost a minute, the boy smiling up at the old man and thanking him.

Then, laughing, the boy raced the doctor downstairs and out to his car. His mother and father followed for the happy farewell.

"Fit as a fiddle!" said the doctor. "Incredible!"

"And strong," said the father. "He got out of his straps himself during the night. Didn't you, Charles?"

"Did I?" said the boy.

"You did! How?"

"Oh," the boy said, "that was a long time ago."

"A long time ago!"

They all laughed, and while they were laughing, the quiet boy moved his bare foot on the sidewalk and merely touched, brushed against a number of red ants that were scurrying about on the sidewalk. Secretly, his eyes shining, while his parents chatted with the old man, he saw the ants hesitate, quiver, and lie still on the cement. He sensed they were cold now.

"Good-by!"

The doctor drove away, waving.

The boy walked ahead of his parents. As he walked he looked away toward the town and began to hum "School Days" under his breath.

"It's good to have him well again," said the father.

"Listen to him. He's so looking forward to school!"

The boy turned quietly. He gave each of his parents a crushing hug. He kissed them both several times.

Then without a word he bounded up the steps into the house.

In the parlor, before the others entered, he quickly opened the bird cage, thrust his hand in, and petted the yellow canary, *once*.

Then he shut the cage door, stood back, and waited.

THE ELECTRONIC WEREWOLF

by Lael Littke and Lori Littke Silfen

Warren began to itch right after he downloaded some information about werewolves from the World Wide Web onto his computer.

At first he thought it was just nervousness because his mom had told him she'd take away his computer privileges if she found him messing around with weird stuff.

But when his eyes began to water and he started coughing, Warren figured he knew what was the matter. His little sister Marcy must have brought home another dog. She was always bringing home strays and begging to keep them even though she knew how allergic he was to dogs. She must have hidden it right here in his room for a while.

When he began to sneeze, Warren decided the dog must still be in the room. He did a thorough search, even under his bed and in the closet. But he didn't find so much as a dog hair.

Even so, he was really ticked off at Marcy.

Sitting down at the computer again he scratched fiercely at the backs of his legs as he scanned the information he'd downloaded. "Lycanthropy," he read. "The assumption of the form of a wolf by a human being." Wow.

Hughie would love this. Hughie was his best friend

who helped him recycle newspapers and aluminum cans to buy computer disks. Hughie loved weird stuff as much as he did. Hughie kept a little notebook in which he wrote down all the strange things the two of them read or heard about.

Warren's eyes skimmed down the list of symptoms of becoming a werewolf. "Paleness," he read aloud. "Clouded vision. Dry eyes. Very dry tongue. Always thirsty. Fear of water."

His throat felt dry and he coughed. Too loud. His mom called out, "War-REN? Are you okay?"

He considered telling her about Marcy bringing a dog, which was making him itch and cough, into his room, but decided the less said at the moment, the better. He wasn't supposed to be using his computer this late at night. There was also the thing about not getting into weird stuff.

"Sure, Mom," he called back. "I'm fine." His voice sounded thick and husky.

Just in case Mom came to investigate, Warren turned off the computer. Tomorrow, he'd read the rest of the file about werewolves. Maybe Mom would be out of the house then.

Walking over to his window, he opened it wide and breathed deeply. A full moon lit the sky, and for a moment he had the urge to go outside and run across the grass. But his mom would ground him for sure if she caught him out at this time of night.

Scratching at his chest, he headed for his bed. There had to be leftover dog hair somewhere in the room, but at least the fresh air would make it possible for him to sleep without sneezing all night long. That Marcy! Had she put the dog in his room deliberately to make him sick? She didn't generally do things like that, but she'd been mad at him for not letting her use his computer.

Well, he'd get even with her in the morning.

The thought made him itch worse.

But even the itching didn't keep him awake. Once he got into bed, he fell asleep almost immediately. He dreamed he sprouted hair on his legs and arms, and that his face elongated into a hairy snout. He dreamed that he got out of bed and leaped from the window. In the light of the full moon, he ran on all fours down the street, his bushy tail streaming behind him.

The dream was scary, and it got even scarier when he loped back to the house, jumped through his window, crept down the hall to Marcy's room, and tore her Barbie doll to bits with his long, sharp teeth.

A screech from Marcy woke him the next morning.

"Mama!" she screamed. "Somebody killed my Barbie!"

Warren, still half asleep, remembered the nightmare. He could almost feel again the crunch of those razor-sharp fangs biting down on the doll.

Frightened, he lay for a moment looking around his room, trying to get his world back into focus. Everything was as it should be. There were his shelves holding his books and the model cars he'd collected when he was a little kid. The big poster showing the earth from space hung just where it should be on his wall. There was the big, oversized wooden pencil he'd won in an essay contest at school. And his desk with his computer was in its usual place.

Looking at the computer made him itch a little, but he ignored it, trying not to think about the night. In his dream it had been *he* who chewed up Marcy's doll.

But it was only a dream. That dog Marcy had brought into the house had done it.

Served her right.

He could hear her sobbing, and Mom and Dad offering soothing words as he got dressed. He almost felt sorry for her when he went out into the hall and she held up the draggled remains of Barbie.

"Look what happened, Warren," she cried.

He went up close. "Too bad, Marcy. Next time don't bring your mangy mutts into the house."

She stared at him, sniffing back tears. "What mutts?"

"You brought a dog into the house yesterday, didn't you?" he asked.

Marcy looked totally bewildered. "I didn't even *see* a dog yesterday. I haven't brought one home since Reginald."

Marcy always gave the strays fancy names.

Dad was looking at Warren. "What makes you think there was a dog in the house yesterday?"

Warren explained about his allergic reactions the night before. He didn't mention anything about the computer or what he had downloaded.

"Are there any signs of a dog in your room?" Dad persisted.

121

Warren shook his head. "Only that I was sneezing and coughing and itching."

Dad walked down the hall and into Warren's room. Warren followed.

Dad looked all around, then paused at the window. "There's a muddy paw print on the sill," he said. "Apparently a dog *did* jump in and chew up Marcy's doll sometime during the day. We're just going to have to keep all the windows shut." Slamming down the window, he locked it.

Warren didn't tell him the window had been shut the whole day until he'd opened it at night.

Marcy calmed down after Mom and Dad promised an elaborate funeral for Barbie when everyone got home that day.

But Warren was troubled as he set off for school. How had that paw print gotten onto his windowsill? *Could* he have changed into some kind of animal? Into a *werewolf*?

No, things like that didn't happen.

He told Hughie about it at noon while they ate their lunches under the elm tree at the far end of the playground. He left out nothing.

"Hey, this is great." Hughie pulled his little notebook from his pocket and started writing in it.

"Is that all you're going to say?" Warren asked. "Hughie, I'm scared."

Hughie continued to write. "Of what?"

"What if it isn't a nightmare? What if it's real?"

122

Hughie thought about that. "Did you say it all started after you downloaded stuff onto your computer?"

"Yeah."

"Then delete it, man. Maybe there's a virus of some kind in what you took off the Web. Maybe it's a werewolf virus. Maybe it got to you." He snickered, but stopped when he saw Warren frown. "Why don't you just delete the whole thing?"

"Think that'll do it?" It sounded too simple for such a major problem.

Hughie shrugged. "If you sprout a tail tonight, you'll know that it didn't." He started writing in his notebook again.

That irritated Warren. Hughie seemed to think it was just some kind of interesting research project.

That afternoon, Warren couldn't concentrate on his schoolwork. During math class he came totally unglued when Mrs. Wellington sent him to the chalkboard. He was supposed to demonstrate one of those complicated problems where a train is traveling at 80 miles an hour and a car is going 60 miles an hour and he had to figure out something or other to keep them from smashing into each other at a crossing.

He stood there at the chalkboard, feeling stupid.

"So what's the answer, Warren?" Mrs. Wellington asked.

"What's the question?"

Mrs. Wellington blinked. "It's not like you to be mouthy, Warren. Just do the problem, please. Write down the figures."

He couldn't even remember what the figures were. He just wanted to get this day over so he could go home and delete that weird stuff from his computer.

"Warren?" Mrs. Wellington sounded stern.

"What?"

"Please demonstrate for us how to set up the problem."

"What *is* the problem?"

"Warren!" Mrs. Wellington said. "You know I don't put up with back talk. I'm going to have to give you a demerit."

"But . . ." he began.

"No buts. Just take your seat and open your book. Then maybe you'll know what problem we're talking about."

Some of the other kids snickered as he sat down. He felt his cheeks grow red.

"I'll get you for that, you old prune," he muttered to himself.

The first thing Warren did when he got home after school was turn on his computer. He clicked quickly to the file about werewolves. It seemed as if there was more than he remembered, pages and pages of were-wolf lore and art. He hadn't realized there were pictures, too. Some of them were scary, showing shaggy werewolves attacking animals and even people. Their eyes were red and their jaws dripped with blood.

As he looked at them, he began to itch. His heart pounded.

"Forget it," he said. He slid the mouse around to tell

124

the computer to deposit the whole thing in the trash can.

The file faded from the screen.

Warren breathed a sigh of relief.

But he continued to itch all during the funeral for Marcy's Barbie doll and the meal at McDonald's afterward, which was Marcy's choice. He tried not to be too obvious about scratching since he didn't want his mom asking too many questions. Even so, he caught her watching him a couple of times.

The second time he managed a little grin.

"Poison ivy," he lied.

She grinned back. "Or maybe too many days between showers."

Had she noticed he hadn't taken a shower that day? For some reason he'd felt afraid of the water.

That night, his room seemed so stuffy that Warren opened the window again. It was all right. He'd deleted the file from his computer. There would be no more muddy paw prints.

But the dream began again immediately after he fell asleep. The long, shaggy hair sprouted along his limbs and he felt his face become a snout. Once again, he leaped from the window and ran down the street.

He knew where he was headed. To Mrs. Wellington's house.

It didn't take him long. He could run much faster on all fours than he could on his usual two legs.

Prowling around her house, he looked for a way to get inside. But everything was locked up tight. He wasn't sure what he would have done if he'd been able to get in. Would he have bitten her? He didn't know.

Her car was in the driveway, that little blue car she depended on to take her to school each morning.

Baring his razor-sharp fangs, he chewed up all four tires, snarling and slavering as his powerful jaws tore at the rubber. It tasted bad, but he didn't care.

Warren didn't tell Hughie everything about that adventure. The next morning on the way to school he just said he'd had the nightmare again. Deleting the werewolf file from his computer hadn't cured whatever it was that was so hideously wrong.

Mrs. Wellington was not in their room when Warren and Hughie arrived. Instead, the principal came and told the class that she would be there in a few minutes and that they should work on their math problems.

Warren's face felt hot, and he began to sweat. Things at home had seemed so normal, with oatmeal for breakfast and sunlight streaming in through the big windows of the kitchen. Warren had told himself that the previous night had not happened.

But when Mrs. Wellington finally walked into the schoolroom and said, with a puzzled look, that the tires of her car had been *chewed*, Warren knew he was in trouble.

The nightmare was real.

All day Warren avoided looking at Mrs. Wellington. And after school, as he walked toward home with

Hughie, he admitted the truth. "I turn into a werewolf at night," he said. "I do bad things."

Hughie regarded him with interest. His hand reached for his pocket where he kept the little notebook, but he stopped when Warren scowled at him and said, "This is serious."

"Sure it is," Hughie said. "But what a great opportunity to do research. How many guys do you know who can shift shapes? You could get on TV, Warren. One of those talk shows."

"I don't want to get on TV," Warren said. "I just want to get back to normal."

Hughie grinned. "Hey, man, maybe being a werewolf is where it's at for you."

Warren felt his face grow hot. "You're starting to bug me, Hughie. Let me tell you something. The last two people who bugged me got something really chewed up."

Hughie's eyes widened. "You mean *you* did the job on Wellington's tires?"

"Yeah," Warren admitted.

Hughie whistled between his teeth. "Okay, man, this *is* serious."

"I told you it was," Warren muttered.

Hughie nodded slowly. "We have to find out what to do about werewolves."

"Without getting rid of *me*," Warren said.

Hughie nodded again. "I'll go home with you. We'll see if we can find something on the Web about how to do it."

Hughie seemed so cheerful that Warren felt his irritation

growing. Hughie probably still thought of the whole thing as something interesting to put in his notebook.

Nobody else was home when they got there. That was good. Warren figured he and Hughie could finish what they had to do before anybody came. But Mom and Marcy would be coming soon.

When Warren turned on his computer, the first thing that came up on the monitor was the stuff about werewolves.

He gasped. "But I deleted the whole file yesterday," he said.

Hughie peered at the screen. "You must have deleted something else, dumb-dumb."

Warren felt his face flame with anger. He began to itch.

"Hughie," he said, "don't rag on me. Look through the stupid file and find out how I can keep from changing into a werewolf." He would have looked himself, but there was something wrong with his eyes. They felt dry—burning, in fact—and it seemed as if he were peering through clouds.

His heart raced suddenly as he realized he'd read that on the list of werewolf symptoms that first night. Cloudy vision. Dry eyes.

Warren tried to swallow, but his tongue was like a desert and stuck to the inside of his cheeks. Confused, he looked out the window, his mind racing. Didn't the moon have to be full in order for him to become a werewolf? It was still late afternoon. There was no moon.

But *something* was going on. The itch was bad, and he had an almost unbearable urge to howl.

Hughie was clicking through pages of information, pausing now and then to examine a picture. "Man," he said. "This is great stuff."

"Forget it!" Warren said hoarsely. "Find the cure!" It was hard for him to speak.

"Okay, okay. Keep your shirt on." Hughie glanced at Warren, then suddenly pushed his chair back. "Hey, man, what's wrong with you? You're pale as milk." He paused, his eyes growing large. "You're not . . . changing, are you?"

"I *told* you," Warren whispered. It was hard to speak. "I *told* you what happens to me." He felt hair sprouting along his arms.

Hughie continued to stare at him. "I'm going home."

"No, you're not." Warren could barely form the words. "Find the cure!"

"I can't find any cures." Hughie turned back to the keyboard, pecking at it with trembling hands.

"Do a search. HURRY!"

"You're making me very nervous, Warren." Hughie tried to rise, but Warren put his hands on his shoulders and pushed him back into the chair.

Only they weren't hands anymore. They were paws. Large, clawed paws covered with dirty, matted hair.

"Warren?" Hughie shrank away from him. "Is that you?"

Warren nodded. His throat hurt, and he didn't try to speak.

Hughie was breathing fast. Turning back to the keyboard, he hit a couple of keys. A sound like a groan came from the computer as the monitor flickered and words appeared.

It seemed to be a poem. Hughie looked at it, then said, "It's like old-time writing. I don't know if I can make it out."

"*Read it,*" Warren snarled.

"Okay, man, okay." Hughie hitched his chair closer and squinted at the screen.

"Even gentle souls, if much provoked,
When anger's fiery flames are stoked,
Can change to wolves by day or night,
Whether full moon's down or shining bright."

He read it all in one breath. Without looking at Warren he said, "Mind if I write that down?"

Warren slammed a hairy paw down on the keyboard. He could no longer speak. His face was elongating, and he could feel sharp fangs forming.

The anger was doing it. Anger at Hughie who, with all that was going on, still acted like this was some sort of game.

Warren eyed the pink flesh of Hughie's arms. He could feel saliva drip from his fangs. "*Hurry,*" he snarled.

"I'm trying," Hughie quavered. "I can't seem to hit the right keys." His hands fumbled at the keyboard. "Hey, I got it now. Look. 'Cures and Solutions for Lycanthropy.'" With one finger he jabbed at the monitor.

It was all a blur to Warren. "Read it!"

"'Milk and whey for three days,'" Hughie gasped.

They didn't have three days. In about three *minutes*, Warren knew, he would no longer be able to keep his fangs off Hughie's flesh.

"'Wormwood,'" Hughie read. "Forget that. 'Draw blood to fainting.'" He looked around at Warren, who shook his shaggy head. No time for that one, either.

"'Final solution,'" Hughie read. "'On rare occasions, victims have been known to track down the werewolf that bit them, though such a search can often take a lifetime to succeed. In such cases, killing the original werewolf has resulted in an immediate end to the curse, freeing the victim—and the entire line of werewolves created by the original—of the taint of evil.'"

"That's no help," Warren gasped. "I wasn't bitten. I don't even know how it happened in the *first* place."

Hughie skipped down to the bottom of the section. "How about this? 'Wooden stake through heart. Also effective on vampires, witches, and other evil entities.' That's the last on the list." Hughie peered fearfully at Warren.

The words came to Warren's ears, but he wasn't sure he understood them. With a great effort he pulled together what wits he still had. Wooden stake. That was his only hope. Otherwise, in about thirty seconds he'd be chewing up the bones of his friend. Then he'd be out the window and who knew what he'd do outside?

Seizing the big, oversized pencil he'd won in the essay contest in his jaws, he dropped it onto the keyboard.

"Do it," he tried to say, but it came out a snarl.

Hughie picked up the big wooden pencil and looked at Warren.

"Do it so I won't tear you apart," Warren said, this time forcing his mouth to form the words clearly enough for Hughie to understand.

Holding the enormous pencil in one hand, Hughie looked around. "There isn't anything here to pound with," he whimpered.

Twitching with longing to crunch Hughie's bones and drink his warm, sweet blood, Warren restrained himself long enough to nudge his heavy dictionary off the shelf where it lay.

Hughie got the idea and picked it up.

Warren made himself place his paws on the computer and stretch upward, giving Hughie a clear shot at his shaggy chest.

Hughie placed the point of the huge pencil against the thick, matted hair. For a moment he hesitated, then suddenly backed away, stumbling over the waste basket and dropping the big pencil and the dictionary.

"I can't do it, buddy," he cried. "I can't do it." He fell to the floor, covering his head with his arms.

A howl of anguish came from Warren's dry throat. Hughie wouldn't use the stake, even to save himself. He couldn't destroy his friend.

Warren turned to Hughie and opened his jaws. He could almost taste the warm, flowing blood. One bite, one tearing chomp, that's all it would take to rip open Hughie's throat.

The throat of his best friend in all the world.

And then, inexplicably, a feeling of calm flowed through Warren like a cool breeze on a hot summer day, and he realized he wasn't—could no longer be—angry at Hughie.

His good friend Hughie, who, for all his joking around, knew how serious this problem was, and had tried to help.

Hughie, who refused to drive a stake through Warren's heart, despite the danger.

Warren closed his jaws, no longer feeling the overwhelming urge to tear his friend apart.

In fact, he felt the werewolf that had been raging to get out suddenly retreat. His snout reshaped itself to become a face. The shaggy hair was replaced by pink skin. The paws became hands.

But he still itched. He might still shift shape again if the anger returned. Something had to be done. He tried to remember what Hughie had read aloud. Something about "ending the line of werewolves."

His gaze drifted over to his computer, its monitor seeming to stare back at the two friends as if it were waiting for something to happen. The computer that, despite Warren's best efforts, refused to free him of this nightmare.

The computer that had, in a sense, infected him, not with a curse, but with a virus.

A werewolf virus.

Warren's eyes grew wide with the realization. He picked up the big wooden pencil and the dictionary Hughie had dropped.

"Hughie," he said gently. "Help me do this."

"What are you doing?" Hughie asked, clearly confused.

"Killing the original werewolf," Warren said.

It wasn't easy to drive the wooden stake through the heart of the computer. It writhed and howled and spurted electronic parts. But the hateful words faded from the monitor's screen.

Warren stopped itching.

His parents would never understand why he'd destroyed his computer. He knew he'd probably not get another until he could earn the money to buy it himself.

He and Hughie sat there quietly for a long time, staring at the ruined computer. Finally, Warren said, "Got any ideas what tires cost? And Barbie dolls?"

Hughie shook his head. "A *lot* of recycled newspapers and pop cans."

Warren sighed. The tires and doll had to be replaced before the computer.

"I'll help," Hughie said.

Warren felt his face changing shape. But not into a snout. Just into a wide smile which he gave to his friend.

WILDING

by Jane Yolen

Zena bounced down the brownstone steps two at a time, her face powdered a light green. It was the latest color and though she didn't think she looked particularly good in it, all the girls were wearing it. Her nails were striped the same hue. She had good nails.

"Zen!" her mother called out the window. "Where are you going? Have you finished your homework?"

"Yes, Mom," Zena said without turning around. "I finished." *Well, almost,* she thought.

"And where are you—"

This time Zena turned. "Out!"

"Out where?"

Ever since Mom had separated from her third pairing, she had been overzealous in her questioning. *"Where are you going? What are you doing? Who's going with you?"* Zena hated all the questions, hated the old nicknames. Zen. Princess. Little Bit.

"Just out."

"Princess, just tell me where. So I won't have to worry."

"We're just going Wilding," Zena said, begrudging every syllable.

"I wish you wouldn't. That's the third time this month. It's not . . . not good. It's dangerous. There have been . . . deaths."

"That's gus, Mom. As in bo-gus. Ganda. As in propa-ganda. And you know it."

"It was on the news."

Zena made a face but didn't deign to answer. Everyone knew the news was not to be trusted.

"Don't forget your collar, then."

Zena pulled the collar out of her coat pocket and held it up above her head as she went down the last of the steps. She waggled it at the window. *That*, she thought, *should quiet Mom's nagging.* Not that she planned to wear the collar. Collars were for little kids out on their first Wildings. Or for tourist woggers. What did she need with one? She was already sixteen and, as the Pack's song went:

> Sweet sixteen
> Powdered green
> Out in the park
> Well after dark,
> Wilding!

The torpedo train growled its way uptown and Zena stood, legs wide apart, disdaining the handgrips. *Hangers are for tourist woggers*, she thought, watching as a pair of high-heeled out-of-towners clutched the overhead straps so tightly their hands turned white from blood loss.

The numbers flashed by—72, 85, 96. She bent her knees and straightened just in time for the torp to jar to a stop and disgorge its passengers. The woggers, hand-combing their dye jobs, got off, too. Zena refused to look at them but guessed they were going where she was going—to the Entrance.

Central Park's walls were now seventeen feet high and topped with electronic mesh. There were only two entrances, built when Wilding became legal. The Westside Entrance was for going in. The 59th Eastside was for going out.

As she came up the steps into the pearly evening light, Zena blinked. First Church was gleaming white and the incised letters on its facade were the only reminder of its religious past. The banners now hanging from its doors proclaimed WILD WOOD CENTRAL, and the fluttering wolf and tiger flags, symbols of extinct mammals, gave a fair indication of the wind. Right now wind meant little to her, but once she was Wilding, she would know every nuance of it.

Zena sniffed the air. Good wind meant good tracking. *If* she went predator. She smiled in anticipation.

Behind her she could hear the tip-taps of wogger high heels. The woggers were giggling, a little scared. *Well,* Zena thought, *they should be a little scared. Wilding is a pure New York sport. No mushy woggers need apply.*

She stepped quickly up the marble steps and entered the mammoth hall.

PRINT HERE, sang out the first display. Zena put her hand on the screen and it read her quickly. She knew she didn't have to worry. Her record was clear—no drugs, no drags. And her mom kept her creddies high enough. Not like some kids who got turned back everywhere, even off the torp trains. And the third time, a dark black line got printed across their palms. A month's worth of indelible ink. *Indelis* meant a month full of no: no vids, no torp trains, no boo-ti-ques for clothes. And no Wilding. *How,* Zena wondered, *could they stand it?*

Nick was waiting by the Wild Wood Central outdoor. He was talking to Marnie and a good-looking dark-haired guy who Marnie was leaning against familiarly.

"Whizzard!" Nick called out when he saw Zena, and she almost blushed under the green powder. Just the one word, said with appreciation, but otherwise he did-n't blink a lash. Zena liked that about Nick. There was something coolish, something even statue about him. And something dangerous, too, even outside the Park, outside of Wilding. It was why they were seeing each other, even after three months, though Zena had never, would never, bring him home to meet her mother.

That dangerousness. Zena had it, too.

She went over and started to apologize for being late, saw the shuttered look in Nick's eyes, and changed her apology into an amusing story about her mom instead. She remembered Nick had once said, *"Apologies are for woggers and kids."*

From her leaning position, Marnie introduced the dark-haired guy as Lazlo. He had dark eyes, too, the rims slightly yellow, which gave him a disquieting appearance. He grunted a hello.

Zena nodded. To do more would have been uncoolish.

"Like the mean green," Marnie said. "Looks coolish on you, foolish on me."

"Na-na," Zena answered, which was what she was supposed to answer. And, actually, she did think Marnie looked good in the green.

"Then let's go Wilding," Marnie said, putting on her collar.

Nick sniffed disdainfully, but he turned toward the door.

The four of them walked out through the tunnel, Marnie and Lazlo holding hands, even though Zena knew he was a just-met. She and Marnie knew everything about one another, had since preschool. Still, that was just like Marnie, overeager in everything.

Nick walked along in his low, slow, almost boneless way that made Zena want to sigh out loud, but she didn't. Soundless, she strode along by his side, their shoulders almost—but not quite—touching. The small bit of air between them crackled with a hot intensity.

As they passed through the first set of rays, a dull yellow light bathed their faces. Zena felt the first shudder go through her body but she worked to control it. In front of her, Lazlo's whole frame seemed to shake.

"Virg," Nick whispered to her, meaning it was Lazlo's first time out Wilding.

Zena was surprised. "True?" she asked.

"He's from O-Hi," Nick said. Then, almost as an afterthought, added, "My cousin."

"O-Hi?" Zena said, smothering both the surprise in her voice and the desire to giggle. Neither would have been coolish. She hadn't known Nick had any cousins, let alone from O-Hi—the boons, the breads of America.

No one left O-Hi except as a tourist. And woggers just didn't look like Lazlo. Nick must have dressed him, must have lent him clothes, must have cut his hair in its fine duo-bop, one side long to the shoulder, one side shaved clean. Zena wondered if Marnie knew Lazlo was from O-Hi. Or if she cared. *Maybe,* Zena thought suddenly, *maybe I don't know Marnie as well as I thought I did.*

They passed the second set of rays; the light was blood red. She felt the beginnings of the change. It was not exactly unpleasant, either. *Something to do,* she remembered from the Wilding brochures she had read back when she was a kid, *with manipulating the basic DNA for a couple of hours.* She'd never really understood that sort of thing. That reminded her of the first time she'd come to Wild Wood Central, with a bunch of her girlfriends. Not coolish, of course, just giggly girls. None of them had stayed past dark and none had been greatly changed that time. Just a bit of hair, a bit of fang. Only Ginger had gotten a tail. But then she was the only one who'd hit puberty, early; it ran in Ginger's family. They'd all gone screaming through the Park as fast as they could and they'd all been wearing collars. Collars made the transition back to human easy, needing no effort on their parts, no will.

Zena reached into the pocket of her coat, fingering the leather collar there. She had plenty of will without it. *Plenty of won't, too!* she thought, feeling a bubble of amusement rise inside. *Will/won't. Will/won't.* The sound bumped about in her head.

When they passed the third rays, the deep green

ones, which made her green face powder sparkle and spread in a mask, Zena laughed out loud. Green rays always seemed to tickle her. Her laugh was high, uncontrolled. Marnie was laughing as well, chattering almost. The green rays took her that way, too. But the boys both gave deep, dark grunts. Lazlo sounded just like Nick.

The brown rays caught them all in the middle of changing and—too late—Zena thought about the collar again. Marnie was wearing hers, and Lazlo his. When she turned to check on Nick, all she saw was a flash of yellow teeth and yellow eyes. For some reason, that so frightened her, she skittered collarless through the tunnel ahead of them all and was gone, Wilding.

The Park was a dark, trembling, mysterious green; a pulsating, moist jungle where leaves large as platters reached out with their bitter, prickly auricles. Monkshood and stagbush, sticklewort and sumac stung Zena's legs as she ran twisting and turning along the pathways, heading toward the open meadow and the fading light, her new tail curled up over her back.

She thought she heard her name being called, but when she turned her head to call back, the only sounds out of her mouth were the pipings and chitterings of a beast. Still, the collar had been in her pocket, and the clothes, molded into monkey skin, remained close enough to her to lend some human memories. Not as strong as if she had been collared, but strong enough.

She forced herself to stop running, forced herself back to a kind of calm. She could feel her human instincts fighting with her monkey memories. The monkey self—not predator but prey—screamed, *Hide! Run! Hide!* The human self reminded her that it was all a game, all in fun.

She trotted toward the meadow, safe in the knowledge that the creepier animals favored the moist, dark tunnel-like passages under the heavy canopy of leaves.

However, by the time she got to the meadow, scampering the last hundred yards on all fours, the daylight was nearly gone. It was, after all, past seven. Maybe even close to eight. It was difficult to tell time in the Park.

There was one slim whitish tree at the edge of the meadow. *Birch,* her human self named it. She climbed it quickly, monkey fingers lending her speed and agility. Near the top, where the tree got bendy, she stopped to scan the meadow. It was aboil with creatures, some partly human, some purely beast. Occasionally one would leap high above the long grass, screeching. It was unclear from the sound whether it was a scream of fear or laughter.

And then she stopped thinking human thoughts at all, surrendering entirely to the Wilding. Smells assaulted her—the sharp tang of leaves, the mustier trunk smell, a sweet larva scent. Her long fingers tore at the bark, uncovering a scramble of beetles. She plucked them up, crammed them into her mouth, tasting the gingery snap of the shells.

A howl beneath the tree made her shiver. She stared down into a black mouth filled with yellow teeth.

"Hunger! Hunger!" howled the mouth.

She scrambled higher up into the tree, which began

to shake dangerously and bend with her weight. Above, a pale, thin moon was rising. She reached one hand up, tried to pluck the moon as if it were a piece of fruit, using her tail for balance. When her fingers closed on nothing, she chittered unhappily. By her third attempt she was tired of the game and, seeing no danger lingering at the tree's base, climbed down.

The meadow's grass was high, and tickled as she ran. Near her, others were scampering, but none reeked of predator and she moved rapidly alongside them, all heading in one direction—toward the smell of water.

The water was in a murky stream. Reaching it, she bent over and drank directly, lapping and sipping in equal measure. The water was cold and sour with urine. She spit it out and looked up. On the other side of the stream was a small copse of trees.

Trees! sang out her monkey mind.

However, she would not wade through the water. Finding a series of rocks, she jumped eagerly stone-to-stone-to-stone. When she got to the other side, she shook her hands and feet vigorously, then gave her tail a shake as well. She did not like the feel of the water. When she was dry enough, she headed for the trees.

At the foot of one tree was a body, human, but crumpled as if it were a pile of old clothes. Green face paint mixed with blood. She touched the leg, then the shoulder, and whimpered. A name came to her. *Marnie?* Then it faded. She touched the unfamiliar face. It was still warm, blood still flowing. Somewhere in the back part of her mind, the human part, she knew she should be doing something. But *what* seemed muddled and far away. She sat by the side of the body, shivering uncontrollably, will-less.

Suddenly there was a deep, low growl behind her and she leapt up, all unthinking, and headed toward the tree. Something caught her tail and pulled. She screamed, high, piercing. And then knifing through her mind, sharp and keen, was a human thought. *Fight.* She turned and kicked out at whatever had hold of her.

All she could see was a dark face with a wide hole for a mouth, and staring blue eyes. Then the creature was on top of her and all her kicking did not seem to be able to stop it at all.

The black face was so close she could smell its breath, hot and carnal. With one final human effort, she reached up to scratch the face and was startled because it did not feel at all like flesh. *Mask,* her human mind said, and then all her human senses flooded back. The Park was suddenly less close, less alive. Sounds once so clear were muddied. Smells faded. But she knew what to do about her attacker. She ripped the mask from his face.

He blinked his blue eyes in surprise, his pale face splotchy with anger. For a moment he was stunned, watching her change beneath him, no longer a monkey, now a strong girl. A strong, screaming girl. She kicked again, straight up.

This time he was the one to scream.

It was the screaming, not the kicking, that saved her. Suddenly there were a half-dozen men in camouflage around her. Men—not animals. She could scarcely understand where they'd come from. But they grabbed her attacker and carried him off. Only two of them stayed with her until the ambulance arrived.

"I don't get it," Zena said when at last she could sit up in the hospital bed. She ached everywhere, but she was alive.

"Without your collar," the man by her bedside said, "it's almost impossible to flash back to being human. You'd normally have to wait out the entire five hours of Wilding. No shortcuts back."

"I know that," Zena said. It came out sharper than she meant, so she added, "I know you, too. You were one of my . . . rescuers."

He nodded. "You were lucky. Usually only the dead flash back that fast."

"So that's what happened to that . . ."

"Her name was Sandra Maharish."

"Oh."

"She'd been foolish enough to leave off her collar, too. Only she hadn't the will you have, the will to flash and fight. It's what saved you."

Zena's mind went, *Will/won't. Will/won't.*

"What?" the man asked. Evidently she had said it aloud.

"Will," Zena whispered. "Only I didn't save me. You did."

"No, Zena, we could never have gotten to you in time if you hadn't screamed. Without the collar, Wild Woods Central can't track you. He counted on that."

"Track me?" Zena, unthinking, put a hand to her neck, found a bandage there.

"We try to keep a careful accounting of everything that goes on in the park," the man said. He looked, Zena thought, pretty coolish in his camouflage. Interesting look-ing, too, his face all planes and angles, with a wild brushy orange mustache. Almost like one of those old pirates.

"Why?" she asked.

"Now that the city is safe everywhere else, people go Wilding just to feel that little shiver of fear. Just to get in touch with their primal selves."

"'Mime the prime,'" Zena said, remembering one of the old commercials.

"Exactly." He smiled. It was a very coolish smile. "And it's our job to make that fear safe. Control the chaos. Keep prime time clean."

"Then that guy . . ." Zena began, shuddering as she recalled the black mask, the hands around her neck.

"He'd actually killed three other girls, the Maharish girl being the latest. All girls without their collars who didn't have the human fight-back know-how. He'd got-ten in unchanged through one of the old tunnels which we should have blocked. *Those wild girls,*' he called them. Thanks to you, we caught him."

"Are you a cop?" Zena wrinkled her nose a bit.

"Nope. I'm a Max," he said, giving her a long, slow wink.

"A Max?"

"We control the Wild Things!" When she looked blank, he said, "It's an old story." He handed her a card. "In case you want to know more."

Zena looked at the card. It was embellished with holo-grams, front and back, of extinct animals. His name, Carl Barkham, was emblazoned in red across the elephant.

Just then her mother came in. Barkham greeted her

with a mock salute and left. He walked down the hall with a deliberate, rangy stride that made him look, Zena thought, a lot like a powerful animal. A lion. Or a tiger.

"Princess!" her mother cried. "I came as soon as I heard."

"I'm fine, Mom," Zena said, not even wincing at the old nickname.

Behind her were Marnie, Lazlo, and Nick. They stood silently by the bed. At last Nick whispered, "You okay?" Somehow he seemed small, young, boneless. He was glancing nervously at Zena, at her mother, then back again. It was very uncoolish.

"I'm fine," Zena said. "Just a little achey." If Barkham was a tiger, then Nick was a cub. "But I realize now that going collarless was really dumb. I was just plain lucky."

"Coolish," Nick said.

But it wasn't. The Max was coolish. Nick was just . . . just . . . foolish.

"I'm ready to go home now, Mom," Zena said. "I've got a lot of homework."

"Homework?" The word fell out of Nick's mouth.

She smiled pityingly at him, put her feet over the side of the bed, and stood. "I've got a lot of studying to do if I want to become a Max."

"What's a Max?" All four of them asked at once.

"Someone who tames the Wild Things," she said. "It's an old story. Come on, Mom. I'm starving. Got anything still hot for dinner?"

JONAS. JUST JONAS

by Nancy Varian Berberick and Greg LaBarbera

Have you ever had a secret?

Then you know how it feels trying to keep one. Your guts feel like they're pressing against you, as if they want to escape the confines of your body. Every moment your throat is tightly clenched because you're afraid the secret will come spilling out.

Some secrets don't really matter, though. When it comes down to it, nobody cares that Sara Downy kissed Johnny Aires in the woods. I wish I had a secret like that. But I don't. My secret is the kind no one can ever know.

I looked away from the wall monitor when my parents walked into the kitchen. My father had his hand-held computer clutched in his grasp. His arm clung around my mother's shoulder. "Have you seen the news this morning, Jonas?"

"No," I answered. The tone in his voice put me on edge and it made me nervous the way my mother kept looking at the floor instead of at me. "Why?" I asked.

"Monitor off," said my father, and the program I'd been watching over breakfast faded as the wall turned to a soft green hue.

They joined me at the table and my father slid his hand-held across the tabletop. For the first time my mother looked at me. Worry lines etched her face. In those lines I read the story of her long battle to accept me the way I am and her struggle to live with the terrible danger I put our family in.

"They found another one, Jonas," my father said. "In Asia."

My hand began to shake as I picked up the palm-sized computer and read the news.

WARRINGTON POST—JUNE 17, 2198. I scrolled down the news file, past the story about last night's strong rains, until the screen showed a picture of a boy no older than my own twelve years. He'd been shot. Then his body had been burned until it looked like charred wood.

I shoved the hand-held away. Closing my eyes, I took a few deep breaths to keep my breakfast from coming back up. When I opened my eyes, my father said gently, "I'm sorry, Jonas. We didn't want you to find out somewhere else."

I nodded but still couldn't speak.

My mother sat still. She reminded me of the holograms we used to download in Mrs. Havacek's sixth grade class, the ones of marble statues from the museums. Without looking up, she whispered, "Maybe we should just move, live someplace so far away no one could ever find out about Jonas."

My father let loose his breath like a huffing bull. "We're not going to live like hermits somewhere in the forest."

That was the worst thing about my life. The hiding. The tension. The keeping of secrets.

All I wanted was for us to live normally, like a regular family. By saying we should move away, my mother took that from me. I watched her staring at the floor. At that moment I wanted to hate her. When she bolted out of the room sobbing, my bitter thoughts turned to sadness. I bit the corner of my mouth to keep my own tears from spilling over.

My father let her go. "Don't worry, Jonas. We're not going to move. No one knows about you. We're safe here."

I thrust my chin toward the window, looking out across the wheat fields glistening in the sun after last night's rain. Right in my line of sight sat a big farm house on the only hill in this flat farm country. Sheriff Conner lived there.

My voice shook. "What about him? He's the worst hater of my kind in town. What if he finds out?"

"Don't worry. Sometimes there's not much for a sheriff to do in a small town, so Conner makes a big deal of other things."

Yeah, but this was a big deal. What I am is the biggest deal in the world.

Look, I don't know a whole lot about it, it's not like we study people like me in school or anything. What I do know is that about a hundred years ago some kids were born with the ability to change their shape. People were hollering "Miracle!" all over the news, at first. When they realized no one could control whether a child would be a Shifter or a Normal, it didn't take long for Normals to become afraid of Shifters. We can do things they can't. Soon after the fear came what scientists called

152

"The Solution." They told everyone that they'd found a way to make sure no one would ever give birth to a Shifter again.

What the scientists said and what's true, though, are two different things. Every now and then one of us still shows up. If we're found out, we're given no mercy. The kid on the morning news-vid learned that.

"Dad," I said, still queasy, "why can't people accept me for who I am? I'm not a bad person!" I squeezed my head with the palms of my hands. "I'm so tired of hiding all the time."

Suddenly the house seemed too closed in. I had to find someplace where I could breathe, where I could forget about my mother's sorrow and the boy burned black as tar. I grabbed my fishing pole from the corner. "I have to get out of here for a while."

"Jonas, try to understand about your mother. She worries about you. It's hard for her."

It was, I knew that. She'd spent all the years of my childhood teaching her little shapeshifting baby not to suddenly turn into a kitten or a puppy or a hand-held computer in front of anyone. It was hard. I naturally wanted to change into anything I saw, or remembered seeing. I didn't understand why I couldn't. She never gave up, and I did learn control and discipline, and to never, ever let anyone know what I am. These lessons had saved my life, but my mother's own life had been a terribly lonely one because of me.

As I hefted my fishing pole and turned to leave, my father put his hand on my shoulder. "Be careful, Jonas."

"I will, Dad."

Free, for a small time, I raced across the yard and into the woods.

I stood in a small clearing, surrounded by tall oaks and maples. My feet squished in grass drenched by last night's rain. Sun streamed down and reflected off a small pool of water. The summer breeze brushed past my face, leaving the scent of pine and earth thick in my nose. I listened and peeked around a few of the trees. Satisfied I was alone, I tossed my fishing pole onto the grass and got ready to Shift.

It's a funny thing, this business of Shifting. Like I said, I don't know how it all works, but I pick up things here and there, on the news or listening to my parents talk. So I do know Shifting has to do with manipulating something called an "energy zone" around my body. Being able to manipulate that zone lets me change shape and it doesn't leave a pile of jeans, underwear, and sneakers behind. Whatever I'm wearing is in the zone and becomes part of the change. Which is good, if you know what I mean.

Kneeling, I sat on my heels and filled my mind with pictures of what I wanted to become. It didn't take long for the change to start reshaping me. My arms pulled in tight to my sides and became wings. My face stretched into a curved beak, and now I saw the world through the eyes of a hawk. In one explosive moment, I screeched and took to the sky. The instant I cleared the treetops I felt whole again.

For a long while I soared over forest and field. Wind sifted through my wing feathers and I floated on currents of warm summer air. If I had a mouth with lips I would have grinned. I could have stayed that way forever but I knew I had to get back. As I glided to the clearing, I noticed a girl walking in the woods on the path that would take her to my house. As high up as I was, my hawk's eyes easily saw her long black hair and I knew her. Here was Angie Conner. My breath felt tingly in my chest. I'd known the sheriff's daughter since before we started kindergarten, but these days I wondered what it would be like if Angie liked me as more than a schoolmate.

It was a painful wondering, because there was so much about me Angie must never know. What kind of friendship can grow on lies?

Angie entered the clearing as my talons grasped the smooth bark of a maple branch. She stopped and looked up at me. Keeping still as she could, she smiled brightly. With all my heart I wished she would recognize me, Jonas, in the hawk's golden eyes. I wanted nothing more than for her to know my secret and accept me for what I am.

She wouldn't, though. She'd be like all the others. If she saw me change shape, that smile would turn to a look of disgust and fear. I couldn't stand the thought of that. My harsh hawk's cry startled her and she jumped back as I spread my wings and let the wind lift me. I didn't look down as I flew toward my house.

Hiding behind the shed, I quickly changed back to Jonas the boy.

A few moments later Angie came out of the woods. She waved and called, "Hi, Jonas! You're just the person I want to see."

"Oh, yeah? What's up?"

I sounded so natural, as though I hadn't seen her only a moment ago. I was very good at using small lies to hide the big secret.

Angie brushed her dark hair back from her cheek. "My dad and Uncle Bill are finished building that fence on the north side of the farm. They asked me to bring the post-hole diggers back to your father. But there are two pairs of them. So I came to see if you'll help me carry them back here."

Would I! I scuffed my toe around on the grass. My heart hammered in my chest, racing with both excitement and fear. The first and last place I wanted to be was at the sheriff's house. First because of Angie. Last because the biggest hater of shapeshifters lived there. But it would be worth the risk to be near Angie. After all, I didn't have to shift shape if I didn't want to. If my mother had taught me nothing else, she'd taught me that.

"Sure, Angie," I said, daring the risk. "Let's go."

We walked back through the woods, down the trail that led to Sheriff Conner's farm. The whole time I watched her out of the corner of my eye, thinking how pretty she was.

Angie caught me looking at her. "What?"

I shook my head. "What do you mean?"

"Why are you staring at me? Do I have something hanging from my nose or something?"

"Well . . . no," I said, laughing. "I just haven't seen you in a while, Angie."

She rolled her eyes and kept walking. "If you'd come around from time to time, you *would* see me."

My heart thumped pleasantly. That was an invitation if ever I heard one! I was glad I was behind her so she couldn't see me grinning like an idiot.

I followed Angie through the woods and out to the narrow path that ran along the edge of her father's fields. In the middle of the largest field a tractor sat angled in the mud. The small, square solar-cell pack hung dangling off the back end and the front left tire was sunk into the muck till half of it was covered in thick black goo.

I whistled. "The rain really messed things up last night."

"Yeah, and to make things worse, the cell-pack is broken and won't recharge. They can't drive the tractor out of the hole. My dad and Uncle Bill have been trying all morning to muscle it out. That's how I got the job of bringing the post-hole diggers back."

I snorted like a pig. "Better than wallowing in the mud with them, I guess."

Angie laughed and led me to the shed next to her house. An old hover-car sat on the paved landing pad. Mrs. Conner's shopping bags were already loaded into the back. We'd just pulled the post-hole diggers from the shed when the screened door opened. Mrs. Conner stood there, wiping her hands on her red-checkered apron.

"Why, Jonas. How nice to see you. You haven't been around in a while."

I smiled and lied. "The chores keep me busy, Mrs. Conner."

"Just like everyone else."

The simple words warmed me. I was not just like everyone else, but it felt good to hear Angie's mom say that.

She flapped her apron at us as though we were chickens in her yard. "Now, you two, before you bring those diggers back, come in for some lunch."

I swallowed hard. A chill raced across my back, like I was thinking about going into a cougar's den asking for a snack.

It'll be all right, I told myself. I remembered my mother's lessons and it seemed I heard her voice in my head, right there as I stood in Mrs. Conner's back yard. *Now remember, Jonas: You don't have to change into anything if you don't want to. You can be Jonas the boy as long as you want to be.*

"Thanks, Mrs. Conner," I said, only a little dry in the mouth. "Lunch sounds great."

When we walked into the dinning room, everyone was already seated around the big table: Sheriff Conner, Angie's uncle Bill, and the sheriff's farm hands, Wes, Jody, and Carl. They shifted around, making room for the guest.

Mrs. Conner came into the dining room with a huge plate of fried chicken, mashed potatoes, and vegetables. As everyone passed the food around, Wes spoke across the table to Angie. "So I see you got a strong man to help you with your chores." He pointed toward me and winked.

Everyone burst out laughing and Angie's Uncle Bill swallowed a mouthful of potatoes and said, "I guess that means you won't be taking her to the junior high dance next year, then, Wes."

Angie rolled her eyes, used to the good-natured teasing.

The laughter settled down to the sounds of everyone eating. Even though the sheriff sat a few chairs away, I had a warm feeling in my stomach. And it wasn't the mashed potatoes, it was the way everyone was treating one another at the table—a wink here, a tease there. Things never felt like this at my house. Dinnertime was always filled with silence and people's eyes focused on their plates. My secret was like a grim guest at the table, forbidding smiles.

I looked over at Angie. My heart started pounding at the thoughts my mind was creating. Maybe this could work out. Maybe I *could* be the one to take her to the dance next year. For a while I lived in my fantasy world, where Angie really liked me, the real me, and her father was no one to be afraid of.

Then Sheriff Conner turned on the wall monitor. A news flash appeared on the screen. A pretty reporter sat behind a desk with a picture of the burned shapeshifter in the upper corner. The screen flashed and buzzed.

"That storm last night sure messed up the town's receiver satellite," said Mrs. Conner.

"Hush, everyone," the sheriff said. "I want to hear what she says."

The reporter read the news quietly, without emotion. "A new report indicates that the thirteen-year-old Shifter had posed as millionaire Ravel Bora's son. The boy had gone into the Bora mansion and stolen many valuable items, including a fifty-thousand-dollar piece of jewelry. He was spotted leaving the premises and caught Shifting in a wooded area nearby."

Mrs. Conner *tsk*ed and shook her head. "He got what he deserved." She passed the potatoes to Angie, who sent them down to me.

Her comment brought grunts of agreement from the men. I passed the potatoes on to the sheriff. My appetite was fading fast. I glanced at Angie, but saw nothing in her expression to say she agreed with her mother or didn't.

A bunch of white spots filled the screen, covering the reporter. The sound went fuzzy so that you couldn't understand a word she was saying.

"Looks like communications will be down for a while," Angie's uncle said.

The sheriff waved his hand and told the monitor to shut down. Scowling, he cut another piece of meat and said, "Serves the Shifter right. *All* of them should be killed. They can't be trusted. Good thing there's none of them in this town because I'd take care of them personally."

My heart stopped for a moment when the sheriff said, "What's the matter, Jonas? You're white as a ghost. Do you feel all right?"

Everyone at the table stopped eating and looked at me. I put my hands in my lap to hide the shaking. The sheriff stared at me with steel blue eyes. I felt sure he read my secret in my face.

I took a deep breath and rubbed my chest, "Yes sir, I'm fine. Just thought something went down the wrong pipe. That's all."

The sheriff crumpled his napkin and dropped it on top of his plate. "Okay everybody, we still have to get that tractor out of the mud and see what's wrong with the solar-cells. Let's get back to work."

The men got up and Mrs. Conner began clearing the table. Angie looked like she was going to help but her mother said, "That's all right, dear. You and Jonas go fetch those post-hole diggers back to his father now."

Angie winked at me, glad to get out of the washing up. I was happier than she was to leave, though she'd never know why. The *bang* of the screen door behind me was the sound of my hopes being accepted among these Normals crashing to the ground.

Angie and I picked up the diggers and hauled them to the narrow road at the edge of the field. Out in the distance, the sheriff and his farm hands stood around the tractor.

"Look," Angie said, "Dad and Uncle Bill have got it moving."

They had, with the sheriff in the driver's seat and Bill guiding Wes and Carl and Jody who were pushing from behind. I took a step closer to the field, squinting to see. Something wasn't right. The tractor lurched forward, but only seemed to be going deeper into the mud. Then I heard them yelling, their voices faint and far away.

Angie's eyes went wide. She screamed "No!" just as the tractor tumbled into a sinkhole and landed on her Uncle Bill, pinning his legs under the wheel.

We flung the diggers away and raced out into the field. By the time we got out to the tractor, mud had caked our legs up past our shoes.

Angie yelled, "Uncle Bill!"

Carl grabbed her and said, "Stay back, Angie."

Wes shouted, "Jonas! Lend a hand!"

I put my shoulder to the front wheel as the men tried to push it off Bill. We might as well have been flies. The huge tractor didn't budge.

"Get away," groaned Bill. "It could go any minute."

At that moment, clutching her apron as she ran, Mrs. Conner reached us. When she saw her brother trapped under the giant wheel, she sobbed, "Oh no, oh, no. Bill!"

Wes pulled a hand-held out of his pocket and punched the codes. After a moment, he shook his head in frustration. "Communications are still down."

Angie slipped her hand into mine and Wes and Jody ran for the hover-car to get help from town. In a few moments we saw them over the fields, Mrs. Conner's shopping bags flying out the windows like white

162

ghosts. They flew low, and then high, and then low again. I knew what that meant—the hover-car was old and not meant for great speed.

Carl and the sheriff did their best to keep Bill comfortable, and Mrs. Conner knelt beside him, brushing his hair off his forehead. Every now and then Bill took a deep breath and squeezed his eyes shut against pain we could only imagine. Whenever he did, Angie's hand in mine tightened to a fist, like she could feel her uncle's agony.

"What's taking so long?" moaned Mrs. Conner, her face streaked with tears.

The sheriff patted her hand. "They just left a few minutes ago, dear. Don't worry. They'll be back as quick as they can."

The tractor groaned and sank further into the mud. Angie screamed. Carl and the sheriff frantically pulled on Bill's arm as the wheel rolled onto his waist and stomach. His eyes grew wide and he shouted, "Get away! Get away!"

Bill's breath came in short, panicky gasps. He kept his hands pressed against the wheel, as if he could keep the weight off of him. The look on the sheriff's face made me realize that they didn't have much time.

My chest tightened and my own breath came quicker. I could fly to town faster than the old hover-car. I could do that, and break my great secret. All my fears came tumbling in on me, fear of being caught and killed. Fear that Angie would look at me with hatred and loathing in her eyes.

It didn't matter. I couldn't let Bill die if there was a chance to save him. Before I could stop myself I said, "I can get to town faster."

The sheriff frowned and said, "How?"

I took a few shaky steps backward. "Promise not to stop me and I'll get help."

Now the sheriff's frown turned to a cold expression, like he was beginning to understand. "What are you talking about, Jonas?"

I knelt in the mud and filled up my mind with pictures of hawks flying. That was all my body needed to remember the proper shape. The change took only a few seconds. Before anyone could cry out, I took to the sky.

Even over my screeching cries, I heard the fear in Angie's voice when she said, "He's a shapeshifter! Jonas is a Shifter!"

I tried to ignore the pain boring into my heart as I pumped my wings and flew toward town. Wind whistled past me as I sped through the air. Below, the road wound like a black river. The white hover-car came into view, flying slow and nowhere near town yet. I left it far behind.

With a hawk's sure grace, I landed in the woods outside of town. I Shifted back to human form and bolted toward the emergency unit squad. A group of people turned toward me as I skidded to a halt. Jane Veigh, the chief of the unit, grabbed my arm, ready to smile if this was some boyish game.

"What's going on, Jonas?" she said, her green eyes twinkling.

"Chief!" I panted. "An accident . . . at the sheriff's place. Bill's pinned . . . pinned under a tractor."

The chief let me go, calling out instructions to her squad. In an instant, the med-flier and a stronger tow-flier zipped out of town. Alone, I stood shaking for a long moment, from my flight and fear. Just as I was beginning to wonder what kind of terrible thing I'd done, the old hover-car put down on the landing pad.

Wes leaned out, a puzzled look on his face. "How did you get here, Jonas?"

I took a step away as Jody yelled, "When we left the Conner place you were there in the field. How'd you get here before us?"

Wes's eyes narrowed. "What's going on here, Jonas?"

Fear took hold of me. My mind filled with images of the hawk flying. *No,* I told myself, *don't change!* I edged backward, trying to make up a story about how I'd gotten a ride into town.

Wes put it together before I could summon the lie.

"He's a Shifter!" he shouted, jabbing his finger at me. "We have to get back and tell the sheriff the boy's a Shifter!"

The hawk's cry screeched across the sky and I felt the wind cold under me before he could shout anything more.

I watched from a perch on a tall pine that overlooked the sheriff's fields as Chief Veigh and her emergency workers pulled Bill from underneath the tractor. Angie

165

and her mother clung to each other as Bill was carefully lifted onto a stretch and put into the med-flier. Once I saw Angie look up to the sky, and then away.

What was she thinking? Did she hate me? Did she wish me dead?

I looked out over the horizon. In one instant my entire life had changed. Our family would have to go into hiding. I watched Angie for a moment. That was as long as I could look at her. I felt as if a stone had dropped, hard and cold, in my stomach. Now I'd never take her to the dance. I couldn't even pretend to be Jonas the boy. I was Jonas the Shifter and the best thing that could happen was that I'd have to leave one life of lies for another.

I lifted my wings to spread them. Then I stopped.

No, I said to myself, inside my head where I am always Jonas no matter what shape anyone else sees. *No, I can't live like this anymore.*

Did I have a plan? Oh yes, a very stupid and dangerous one. I decided I'd rather die than live with secrets again, because living a lie was just the same as being dead. The time had come to really live, even if it meant I wasn't going to live long.

I lifted off the tree limb and glided back toward the field.

Hawks can see mice from cloud-high and hear them squeak. Gliding over the fields I saw Bill and the emergency team leave just before Wes and Jody arrived. I didn't see Mrs. Conner, and I knew she must have gone with her brother. Angie stood alone outside the group of farmhands, looking small and frightened as her father reached into the tractor and pulled out a long laser-rifle. Like every farmer, he kept it there in case he crossed paths with a snake. I knew he figured he'd done that today.

"We're going to take care of that Shifter," he said, checking the rifle's load. "And we'll take care of those parents of his, too."

Wes spat. "They're traitors! Hiding a Shifter—how do we know they're not Shifters, too? I'll go into town to get some more men, Sheriff."

Sheriff Conner stopped him. "No. Stay here. No one knows about this but us, and I don't want people running all over the town, shooting at chickens and dogs every time they think they've spotted the Shifter. I'll take him down."

Angie looked up and saw me. Swallowing hard, just like she was scratching up her courage, she stepped in front of her father.

"Dad," she said, "you're wrong."

The sheriff's face flushed red. "Wrong? About what? About a cowardly traitor to the human race?"

Angie pointed up to me, the hawk gliding on the warm currents. "Jonas isn't a coward, Dad—"

My heart almost stopped when the sheriff looked up. He raised his rifle, and Angie jumped to drag his arm down. "No! I'm telling you he's no coward! He's here, isn't he?"

She lifted up her arm, high and straight, like a

167

huntress calling down her hawk. Terrified, and unable to go back, I dropped down. I landed on her arm as though we'd done this a hundred times. The farm hands stepped back, but Sheriff Conner held his ground.

"Don't change shape," Angie whispered to me.

No problem, I thought. I wanted my wings to fly if I had to.

"Dad," she said, "listen. If Jonas was a coward, he wouldn't have come back. And if he was a traitor he wouldn't have risked his life—and his parents' lives!—to help Uncle Bill."

The sheriff looked at me with disgust. "He's not a Normal, Angie. He's one of those . . . things." He lifted his rifle. "Now, get away from him."

Angie held her ground, but I felt her trembling. She'd used her best argument and it hadn't made any difference. I needed my voice to speak for myself now, and to get it I'd have to give up my wings. Images of Jonas the boy flooding into my mind, I hopped from Angie's arm. I wore human shape as my feet hit the muddy ground.

The sheriff lifted his rifle to sight. Angie jumped in front of me, shouting, "No! Don't shoot him!"

I put my hands on her shoulders and gently moved her aside.

"Sheriff Conner," I said, "I've never done anything to hurt anyone. You've known me all my life and you know that. My parents are good people and they've taught me the same things you've taught Angie. I don't steal and I don't cheat." I pressed my hands to my chest. "I am who I am—and that's always Jonas."

The sheriff looked at me for a long time, his eyes boring into me like he wanted to see right into my heart. Only a few hours ago I'd wanted Angie to look into the hawk's eyes and see Jonas there. Just Jonas, as I always am. I'd wanted that a lot then, but not nearly as much as I wanted the sheriff to see me now. Silence stretched on for what seemed like hours. Angie covered my hand with hers, offering comfort and courage. Maybe that gesture made the sheriff lower his rifle. Or maybe he did see the real truth of who I am: Jonas. Just Jonas.

"Boy," he said, his voice hoarse and gruff with feeling. "I can't deny you did a good thing here today. My wife's brother is a fine man, and he would have died if it wasn't for you." His steely eyes narrowed. "But I can't deny you're a Shifter, either."

I nodded, still afraid. "Neither can I, Sheriff. Not anymore."

He smiled at that, just a little quirk of his lips, and Angie squeezed my hand.

"Dad," she said, her voice shaky, "do you think we can go back to the house now and see if Mom's come home with news about Uncle Bill?"

The sheriff glared at me, and then over his shoulder at the four farm hands. "Not yet," he said grimly. "There's still something we need to do."

My mouth dried up with sudden fear.

"Listen, everyone here: Promises are going to be made, and they are going to be kept. Jonas!"

"Yes, sir?" I could hardly squeak out the words.

"Swear to me, boy, on your own life, that you'll never shift shape around me or mine."

On my own life, I swore.

"Wes! Carl! Jody!"

They stepped forward, puzzled and uneasy. "Yes, sir."

"Jonas risked his life here today, and that has to count for something. Swear to me, right now, right here, that you'll never tell anyone what you know about him."

Carl winked at me and gave his oath, easily and at once. Jody muttered that he reckoned it could have been him under the tractor's wheel if things had been a little different. Wes kicked at the mud and agreed.

"Now," said the sheriff, "let's go see if there's any news about Bill."

We trooped across the muddy field, the men in front and Angie and I behind. She hadn't let go of my hand all the while the oaths were being made, and she didn't let go till we got back to the farmhouse.

In the yard, she took her hand from mine and said, "It isn't going to be easy, Jonas. My dad and the others will keep their promises. I know Mom and Uncle Bill will, too. But you have to be very careful. People must never, ever know."

That's what my mother had taught me, and I know I should have remembered her warning. But I'd gained too much in the risk to regret having taken it.

A real life, a friend I didn't have to lie to, and the acceptance of a very few people who, if they don't understand me, at least accept me as Jonas, just Jonas.

Shifters don't get that in this life. Not ever. For these things I'd have done it all again.

A MILLION COPIES IN PRINT

by John C. Bunnell

Y ou know the books. You devour them like M&Ms and collect them like pack rats. Grown-ups grumble about them to each other, and complain that you ought to be reading *Moby Dick*, or at least *Treasure Island*. But the books still sell millions of copies apiece, the series gets longer and longer—and yet somehow it always seems as if there are more copies lying around than there are kids to read them.

That's because there are. And it's not for the reason you think.

First of all, nothing you've read about the author is true. Oh, he's a real person, but he doesn't write the books. He might even admit that these days if you pried his phone number out of the right computer and called him up. There are other writers around who'll tell you they write the books for him, but they're lying, all of them. Those other writers even lie to each other about not being paid enough to ghostwrite the stories. They get paid really well to tell those lies; it's one of the sneakier parts of the whole setup.

The truth is that it's all a plot to take over your world. I know, because my brother is running it.

That's right, I said "your" world. I can't tell you where ours is. You haven't named the star yet, and the scientific reference number attached to it wouldn't mean anything to most of you.

We were separated when our spaceship crashed on your planet a number of years ago, and for a long time I didn't know my brother had survived. We'd gone down in separate lifepods, and there was no practical way for me to track him down. We're natural chameleons, you see—we can change shape to blend in with our surroundings. If he'd survived the landing, there was no telling what he might have turned into in order to escape being locked up by a UFO buff or a government scientific team. Me? I've spent the last dozen or so years as a succession of house pets: cats, ferrets, mynah birds and so forth. It's the best way I've found to learn about a culture while someone else sees to your food, shelter, and well-being.

Arel had a different idea. He's always liked being in control of things. When he was in our equivalent of third grade, he convinced three entire first grade classes to turn themselves into *kaia* pieces so he could play a practice game with himself. (*Kaia* is much like your chess, only there are fifty pieces on each side, and games often last a day or more.) A minor annoyance, true, and not exactly the kind of behavior you'd associate with would-be world conquerors later in life, but they have to start somewhere, don't they? Believe me— as Arel got older, his plans became far more complicated—and sinister—which only made things worse for everyone back home.

Knowing Arel as I do, I've often wondered if the

crash of our ship was *really* an accident, or if he'd grown bored with our homeworld and needed a new planet where he could continue his special brand of troublemaking.

As for me, I've always been too busy staying alive to pick up on what he'd done here until the scheme had been running for a while.

At the time, I was a cat, and the human who'd adopted me ran a used bookstore. One night I happened to stroll through the section of kids' books, and all of a sudden there they were: a half-dozen of *those* books. And they were glowing.

Well, not exactly glowing, at least not so humans could see. It's like this: when you're a natural chameleon, you have to be able to find other chameleons. In our case, we give off a particular sort of light, way down the spectrum where you can only see it if you have exactly the right kind of eyesight. That little group of books was giving off just that kind of light, and for a moment I thought someone might actually have sent a rescue ship out to look for us.

No such luck. When I looked more closely, I realized the books weren't other chameleons after all. The auras weren't bright enough, for one thing. And of course if they'd been a rescue team, they'd have changed into more useful shapes once the store had closed and there was no one else around to see. I shifted out of cat form just enough to bring my senses up to full strength, and started to reach for one of the books. But just before my hand made contact, I realized what the books really were and jerked it back so fast I fell over backward.

They were humans—human children—who'd been shifted into the shapes of books and frozen that way.

Yes, we can do that. Scientists back home claim our ancestors learned how to contact-shift way back when we were hunter-predators. We don't use the ability much anymore, though, and it's degenerated over the last thousand years. Now we need amplifying gear to force a change on anything much bigger or more complicated than a loaf of bread. There was an amplifier in our spaceship, but the ship had burned up in Earth's atmosphere. So the fact that a half-dozen shift-victims were sitting on a bookshelf in front of me meant two things: Arel had survived, and he'd brought the amplifier down in his lifepod. The question was why, and as I studied the "books" as carefully as I could without touching them, I tried to work out an explanation.

As I did so, I discovered that the situation was even stranger than I'd imagined. The energy auras of the shapechanged books were dimmer than mine or Arel's. But they were also somehow more intense. There was too much dormant energy trapped in those "books," and without proper equipment, it was hard to tell what it was doing there. One worrisome possibility did occur to me, and I could think of only one way to test it. So I shifted back to cat form and slipped quietly out of the kids' aisle and back to the stockroom, going into hunter-predator mode myself.

Despite three lives as a cat, I've never been much of a

mouser, and it took me most of two hours to find a mouse and catch it. The last half hour was the hardest, because I didn't want to kill the mouse, and I had to work out how to stun it so I could pick it up and carry it back to the kids' section. Eventually, though, I trotted into the proper aisle, mouse in mouth, and walked up to the shelf with the shapechanged books in it. Fortunately, it was a bottom shelf, so I could reach it without having to stretch. I shook my head back and forth a couple of times, batting the mouse's nose with a paw to make sure it was still alive. Then, with a mighty toss, I opened my mouth and threw the mouse at my target.

Considering that it was nearly impossible to aim, I didn't do badly. The mouse struck the row of books at the right edge of the cluster of chameleon-victims, and had just enough time to squeak angrily at me before it was caught by exactly the effect I'd suspected. There was a faint flash of "light"—again, something I could see but no human could detect—and by the time the mouse hit the floor, it wasn't a mouse anymore. Instead, it was an exact duplicate of the sixth changed "book" in the row, right down to the grape juice stain at the bottom of the spine. We can't do that kind of relayed shapeshifting by ourselves, but you can program an amplifier for it. And if the target object (or mouse, or person) isn't a chameleon, it's stuck in whatever form it's been turned into.

If you've learned about conservation of energy, you might think the relay effect couldn't be passed from one victim to another. In this case, though, you'd be wrong. When a ten-year-old human turns into a book, eighty-odd pounds of matter vanish by turning into energy; less than a pound of it reappears in the book. Most of it is stored as potential energy—more than enough to activate any triggering codes, which would be copied onto the new "book." The closest concept I've come across on your planet is the computer virus. I trust you can see the parallel.

There was nothing I could do for the frozen youngsters without an amplifier of my own. But since I now knew what to expect, I could allow Arel's effect to change me, "read" the trigger conditions, and then shift out of book form using my own abilities. At least I *should* be able to change back. It was barely possible that Arel had coded the book pattern to block shifting ability in a changed target. In that case, I'd be in as much trouble as the other six victims on the bookshelf. Not to mention the mouse.

But that prospect seemed unlikely, and I decided it was worth the risk. So I took a deep breath, lifted a paw again, and reached out to touch one of the other shapechanged books.

The sensations that washed over me were half familiar, half frightening. The change itself was no surprise, but there was a terrifying quality about shifting without being in control of the process. I could feel myself turning from flesh and muscle and bone to paper and glue and ink, and it *hurt*. More, the amount of energy tied up in the prior victim's mass was considerable. There was too much for me to do more than ride out the transformation, and it occurred to me that it might overload my own cells' ability to shift. Yet the process was also amazingly fast, and before I'd had time to fully form that thought, I'd become yet another paperback book lying on the floor next to the former mouse.

Tentatively, I flexed my mental faculties to see if all of me was still there and in working order. Everything seemed all right, but I didn't relax until I'd done several tests. First I tried to change the volume number on the book's spine from "24" to "19": success. Then I tried fiddling with the number of pages, absorbing the mass of the ads in the back of the book into the covers. Again, success, though it took more effort than I'd expected. Finally, I experimented with the cover, trying to change the pumpkin head in the garish illustration into a genuine, 3-D pumpkin. When that last trick worked, I breathed a psychic sigh of relief and settled down to take a thorough look at the state of my innards and the codes I'd inherited from Arel's amplifier programming.

By the time I shapeshifted back into cat form an hour and a half later, I was incredibly tired. I was also incredibly shocked. I'd been very lucky. There were several separate trigger conditions, designed to limit the transformations to living creatures, preferably humans. The trick with the mouse had only worked because no one else had been around, and I'd hit the book hard enough for the stored energy to register the impact.

There was more. As far as I could tell, the "book" that had zapped me was at least a seventeenth-generation copy. And every reader caught in a shift gave the next book the power to trigger at least a dozen fresh shapechanges. Even as a cat, I knew the books Arel was using were absurdly popular. It didn't take much math to work out that there had to be a spectacular number of young humans locked into book form and scattered all over the planet.

But the worst of it was that I couldn't think of a single thing I could do about any of it.

It's been over two years since that night, and the only reason humanity is still in charge of this planet is that you people breed alarmingly fast, and more and more families are arriving in this part of the world every week.

I've been trying to trace Arel's path backward so I can figure out where he landed. If I could get to his amplifier, or even his lifepod, I might be able to start turning some of the shapechanged books back into humans—at least the ones that haven't been recycled, chewed up by dogs, or dropped down storm drains and ruined. But so far all the leads I've checked run into dead ends. Arel's covered his tracks very well, and every time I think I've gotten close, he disappears again.

In the meantime, I figure the best I can do is to try and warn you about what's going on. Arel's not likely to see this—he was never much of a reader back home, and I doubt that's changed much here, given that you still haven't developed holographic media.

Unfortunately, I can't name the series he's sponsoring. The editors of this book tell me that would be trademark infringement, or libel, or maybe both. (I'm pretty sure they think this story is pure fiction anyway, but you'll know better. You've seen how *those* books multiply.)

So be careful. I think Arel may be branching out. I was browsing in a bookstore in Colorado last month, and a new series of TV tie-in novels for teenaged girls caught my eye. I thought one copy of the third book might be a shapechanged human, but someone bought it before I could get a good look.

And of course, if he ever gets hold of a copy of *Bruce Coville's Shapeshifters* and reads it, all bets are off.

ABOUT THE AUTHORS

LAWRENCE WATT-EVANS is the author of a couple of dozen novels and over a hundred short stories, and more than half a dozen that have appeared in previous Bruce Coville anthologies. He's a full-time writer living in Maryland with his wife, two kids, a cat, and a hamster.

MARK A. GARLAND has spent the last dozen years reading, going back to school, attending conventions, and writing. His works include *Dinotopia* and *Star Trek* books, as well as his original novel *Sword of the Prophets* and nearly fifty published short stories, poems, and articles. Mark lives in upstate New York with his wife, their three children, and (of course) a cat.

JANNI LEE SIMNER grew up on Long Island and journeyed west as soon as she could. She currently lives in the very un-swampy Arizona desert, which was the setting for her bestselling *Phantom Rider* trilogy. Her short stories have appeared in more than two dozen anthologies and magazines, including *A Starfarer's Dozen*, *A Glory of Unicorns*, and *Bruce Coville's Book of Nightmares*.

SUSAN J. KROUPA has made up stories since she was a small child, but had teenagers of her own before she got around to writing the stories down. Her work has appeared in various anthologies and in *Realms of Fantasy*. Susan lives in Orem, Utah, with her husband and children, in a household ruled by a hound/German shepherd mix named Tiyo.

ANNE MAZER grew up in a family of writers in upstate New York. Her work includes *The Salamander Room*, *Moose Street*, and *The Oxboy*. Anne lives in Ithaca, New York, with her son, Max, and daughter, Mollie.

JESSICA AMANDA SALMONSON has published over 200 short stories and poems, and is the author of such novels as *The Disfavored Hero*, *Thousand Shrine Warrior*, and *The Swordswoman*, as well as the reference work *The Encyclopedia of Amazons*. She lives in Seattle, Washington, with artist Rhonda Jean Boothe, together with their pet ratties and salamanders.

JACK DANN has written or edited over fifty books—including the international bestseller *The Memory Cathedral*—and is the recipient of the Nebula

Award, the Australian Aurealis Award (twice), the Ditmar Award, and the Premios Gilgames de Narrativa Fantastica award. Jack lives in Melbourne, Australia, and "commutes" back and forth to Los Angeles and New York.

CONNIE WILKINS lives in the 5-college area of western Massachusetts, where she co-owns two stores supplying the non-essential necessities of student life. On buying trips to New York she always pays her respects to the stone wolves, who really do look down from high above W. 30th Street. Her stories have appeared most recently in *Marion Zimmer Bradley's Fantasy Magazine* and the Daw anthology *Prom Night*.

RAY BRADBURY lives in Los Angeles. He sold his first story over fifty years ago, when he was only twenty. Still actively writing, he is beloved throughout the world as one of the most poetic science fiction writers of all time.

LAEL LITTKE is a full-time writer who lives in Pasadena, California, with six cats and two dogs. She has more than thirty books for young people to her credit, including her latest, *Haunted Sister*. She loves to write short stories now and then, especially the strange ones she and her daughter, Lori Littke Silfen, work on together.

LORI LITTKE SILFEN lives near San Diego, California, with her husband, Douglas, her cat, Tora, and also two computers, which inspire her to create magical stories. By day, Lori works as a technical writer.

JANE YOLEN has published more than a hundred and seventy books. Her work ranges from the slap-happy adventures of Commander Toad to such dark and serious novels as *The Devil's Arithmetic* (which was made into a Showtime movie), to the space fantasy of her much-beloved *Pit Dragon Trilogy*. She lives in a huge old farmhouse in western Massachusetts with her husband, computer scientist David Stemple.

NANCY VARIAN BERBERICK has written stories with Greg LaBarbera for two other Bruce Coville anthologies: *Ghosts II* and *A Glory of Unicorns*. Nancy also writes fantasy fiction for grown-ups; her latest novel is *Tears of the Night Sky*. Nancy lives with her husband, architect Bruce A. Berberick, and their two dogs, Pagie and Piper, in Charlotte, NC.

GREG LaBARBERA lives in Charlotte, North Carolina, with his wife, Jackie, and their three black Labradors. Besides writing stories for young people, Greg enjoys writing songs and playing guitar in his rock band Small Time Joe. "Jonas. Just Jonas" is his third published story with collaborator Nancy Berberick.

JOHN C. BUNNELL lives and writes in Oregon. His stories and reviews have appeared in *Bruce Coville's Book of Aliens II*, and in magazines such as *Dragon*, *Duelist*, *Sci-Fi Entertainment*, and *Amazing Stories*. He notes that, as in his story "A Million Copies in Print," there are a lot of "those" books on the shelves at one of the nation's biggest bookstores, located not far from his home. . . .

ABOUT THE ARTISTS

ERNIE COLÓN, cover and interior artist, has worked on a wide variety of comic book-related projects during the course of his long career, including graphic novels, comic strips, and various superhero titles. His many artistic accomplishments include *John Carter: Warlord of Mars*, *Doom 2099*, and *Damage Control* for Marvel Comics; *Arak: Son of Thunder*, *Underworld*, and the epic maxi-series *Amethyst, Princess of Gemworld* for DC Comics; and *Magnus, Robot Fighter* for Valiant Comics. His work in children's comics includes *Rocky and Bullwinkle*, *Mighty Mouse*, and the *Star Wars* tie-in *Droids* (Marvel); *Scooby Doo* (DC); *Richie Rich* and *Casper, the Friendly Ghost* (Harvey); and the mysteriously titled *Wham-O Giant Comics*. Ernie lives in Long Island, New York, with his wife and daughter.

JOHN NYBERG, who inked the story illustrations, has been a comic book artist for 14 years. Among his many accomplishments are *Green Arrow*, *Plastic Man*, and *The Flash* for DC Comics; *Doom 2099* for Marvel; and *WildC.A.T.S.* and *C-23* for Image. He also provided the illustrations for the young-adult novel *Spider-Man Super Thriller: Deadly Cure*. The highlight of his career has been working with his three favorite comic book artists: Steve Rude, José Luis Garcia-Lopez, and Kevin Nowlan. He was nominated for a Kirby Award in the category of "Best Art Team" with Steve Rude for the series *Nexus*, and a Harvey Award and an Eisner Award in the category of "Best Inker." John lives in New Jersey with his wife, Amy, and their two cats, Bart and Lisa.

BRUCE COVILLE was born in Syracuse, New York, and grew up in a rural area north of the city, around the corner from his grandparents' dairy farm. He lives in a brick house in Syracuse with his wife, his youngest child, three cats, and a dog named Thor. Though he has been a teacher, a toymaker, and a gravedigger, he prefers writing. His dozens of books for young readers include the bestselling *My Teacher Is an Alien* series, *Goblins in the Castle*, *Aliens Ate My Homework*, and *Sarah's Unicorn*.